SERGIO Y.

Alexandre Vidal Porto

SERGIO Y.

*Translated from the Portuguese
by Alex Ladd*

Europa
editions

Europa Editions
214 West 29th Street
New York, N.Y. 10001
www.europaeditions.com
info@europaeditions.com

Copyright © 2015 by Alexandre Vidal Porto
First Publication 2016 by Europa Editions

Translation by Alex Ladd
Original title: *Sergio Y. Vai à América*
Translation copyright © 2015 by Europa Editions

Library of Congress Cataloging in Publication Data is available
ISBN 978-1-60945-327-5

Vidal Porto, Alexandre
Sergio Y.

Book design by Emanuele Ragnisco
www.mekkanografici.com

Cover photo © sebastian-julian/iStock

Prepress by Grafica Punto Print – Rome

Printed in the USA

For Michael B.

What is then between us?
What is the count of the scores or hundreds of years between us?
—WALT WHITMAN, *Crossing Brooklyn Ferry*

And just as you felt everything, I feel everything,
and here we are holding hands,
Holding hands, Walt, holding hands,
the universe dancing in our souls.
—FERNANDO PESSOA, *A Salute to Walt Whitman*

CONTENTS

SERGIO Y.

ALL YOU NEED KNOW ABOUT ME

For our vanity is such that we hold our own characters immutable and we are slow to acknowledge that they have changed, even for the better.
—E. M. FORSTER

S ince I mean to speak of the lives of others, it is only fair that I speak of mine.

My name is Armando. I turned seventy last month. Generally, people think I am older. It has been that way my entire life. I have come to expect it when I meet someone for the first time. I appear older than I am. This visible premature aging is common among psychiatrists. We absorb our patients' problems. We grow old for them.

I am one of the city's best doctors. It may sound immodest, I know, to refer to myself in such a manner, but that is how I am referred to when my work is mentioned. I am proud of the recognition I have earned over the years. I am vain, but it does not bother me. I have always thought modesty an overrated quality.

I realize vanity can be a treacherous thing. I think, however, that in my life, it has played a constructive role. My vanity has meant I have rarely found it necessary to diverge from the natural dictates of my will. As a professional, I have opted not to make compromises. I have approached my profession on my terms. Things might not have worked out. But fortunately they did.

My father was also a doctor. When I was a child, I liked to watch him get into his car in the morning to go to the hospital. In my child's mind, knowing he was a doctor meant my family and I were shielded from pain or death. It gave me a sense of security. When we ran into people who knew him, I was proud of the respect and deference they showed him.

I wanted to be a doctor just like him. I grew up idolizing him. My father died in a stupid traffic accident when he was forty-eight. I had just turned sixteen. After his death, my desire to be a doctor only became stronger and deeper.

And that is what I did.

In 1967, I obtained my degree from the University of São Paulo's Medical School as a member of its fiftieth graduating class. I was at the top of my class, every year, beginning my freshman year. I did my residency in the United States and returned to Brazil for my PhD. After that, I took the necessary exams and obtained my teaching credentials. I started as an associate professor of medical psychology. I retired as department chair.

In addition to my academic responsibilities, I have always treated a varying number of private patients. Throughout the years I have had good results. I think I have helped some people.

My father, Miguel, was my mother Ondina's first boyfriend. She was widowed at forty-five and never remarried. When she died, she was a year younger than I am now. From the time she became a widow until I graduated from college, a day did not go by when she did not visit Alba and Yeda, her two sisters, who lived together in an old house in the Moema neighborhood.

At 11:30 A.M. Joel, the driver, would drive her to my aunt's house on Jauaperi Street. The three women would sit down for lunch. Then they would sit on the couch and watch television. Every day, they would sip their coffees while watching the news and then the featured film for that afternoon, whatever that might be.

Around 4:30 P.M., Maria José, the maid, would serve them more coffee, this time with a slice of cake, cookies or whatever other treats were in the kitchen that day. Sometimes, instead of staying at home, they would go to the mall or to a doctor's appointment. Joel would drive them, and they would all ride in the backseat together.

When I moved to New York for my residency, my mother temporarily moved in with her sisters. She never moved back. Ondina, Alba and Yeda lived together on Jauaperi Street until they died.

They vanished, one by one, like birds, over a space of ten months. The first to go was Alba, hit by a motorcycle courier while she hailed a taxi in front of the bank where she collected her pension. She died in January. The second to go was my mother, who had been diagnosed with pancreatic cancer at the end of the previous year. She passed away in May. Yeda, the last one to go, suffered a stroke in the middle of the night and never woke up to see August 19th.

I am also a widower. My wife, Heloísa, died nearly seven years ago. After her death, my most palpable feeling was one of relief. It hurt to see her slowly wasting away in the hospital. To shield myself from the pain, about a month before her actual death, in my own mind, I declared her dead. I killed her before she died. But, all along, I was by her side, until her heart finally stopped beating.

I have managed to move on. I lead a normal and satisfactory life. I do not feel alone. But it bothers me to talk about the fact that I am a widower. Not because it moves me or makes me sad. It is just the opposite. I think it should move me more. This is what disturbs me.

My marriage, which lasted thirty-seven years, was a happy one. In the photo on the dresser in the bedroom we shared together, it still is a happy marriage. But now that picture of my wife is enough for me. It suffices.

I may seem cold, even contemptible, but if I lay bare my feelings in this way it is only to show my sincerity and good faith in writing this report.

Heloísa and I had only one child, Mariana, who is now an adult and lives in Chicago. She married an American she met while getting her master's. I have no grandchildren yet.

Since Mariana left home to study abroad, four years after her mother died, I have lived alone in a four-bedroom apartment on Ceará Street, in Higienópolis in São Paulo, in the same house where the three of us once lived.

With my marital obligations concluded and my parental ones suspended, patients have come to occupy a larger space in my life. Nowadays, I do not know what I would do without them. If all of them were to disappear, wiped out by some plague, let us say, I could probably find things to do. I would not die of boredom. But the truth is I need to define what I will do when the day comes and I have no one left to treat.

The most natural thing would be for me to move to the beach house, which is where most of my books are. However, I know that I will be here for as long as I still have patients in São Paulo, because nothing in life gives me more pleasure. When my mother complained that my father saw too many patients, he answered: "A doctor without a patient is a nobody." I agree.

It is in my patients that I find the raw material for my life's major achievements. I care for them as best I can. I get involved in their cases. For each one of them, I read, I reflect, I give of myself. I try to understand what pains them. I ponder it at length. I am meticulous. I take my time in reaching my conclusions.

If I were not careful, my life would be overwhelmed, consumed by the personal problems of others. I would look even older than I do now. To avoid this, I now see only five patients. One a day, Monday through Friday. This allows me to organize my time more efficiently.

I used to take detailed notes of each session. However, ever since I was diagnosed with early arthritis in my right hand, that has changed. Christmas 2003, my daughter gave me a digital recorder, one of those that do not need cassette tapes. From then on, I have only jotted down generic notes while discreetly recording sessions for future reference.

This allowed me to calmly recopy my notes after each session. This change made my work more consistent. I could play back the recordings as many times as I wished. I could hear the pauses, the silences. I could perceive changes in the breathing. I gained elements of analysis that the previous method of note-taking did not offer me.

Whenever my interest in a patient began to wane, I would try to discharge them as soon as possible. In such situations, my logic went something like this: I do not want to devote my time to this patient, therefore he does not need me. He will be better off with someone else.

There were times, though, when a case genuinely interested me and, for reasons beyond my control, I could not arouse the patient's interest in being treated. When this happened, I was the one who was discharged.

When a patient left me, I would feel a deep sadness: infantile and unjustifiable. Something similar to the impotence a child feels when he discovers another child, younger than him, has broken his favorite toy, and that there is nothing that can be done about it.

Whenever I took interest in the case and the patient also showed interest in the therapy, at some point, I would invariably become obsessed. My obsession persisted for as long as the mystery lasted for me. It would last for as long as I could lose myself in the case in my attempts to understand it.

Some obsessions were easily overcome. Others, however, haunted me for years, even after the patient-therapist relationship had ended. I believe this is what happened with Sergio Y.

With him, I learned that some patients realize before the doctor when the optimal point in their treatment has been reached—when to stop, the moment when the returns start diminishing. It was with Sergio that I discovered the importance of humility.

I never did understand, however, in this story that I am about to tell, whether somebody in fact abandoned somebody else.

I want to make clear that, at this point in my life, I have no desire to lay bare the intimate details of a person who has entrusted his privacy to me. However, if I comment on this case and am somehow remiss with regard to my professional oath, my reasons for doing so have great merit.

It is true: I have not kept secret what my eyes have seen and my ears have heard. I know. But I do have principles. My intention in telling this story is not to do harm. I want to become a better doctor and a more principled human being. My intent is to learn.

The patient I will speak of came to my office recommended by his school principal, a friend of mine from college. In her e-mail, she said a seventeen-year-old student, "articulate, intelligent and confused," would call. According to her, it was an "interesting case."

I took note of that.

THE INTERESTING PATIENT

It was a very hot day in São Paulo. On the streets that morning people walked around hoping rain would come and cool things off. No one imagined, though, that it would grow dark so suddenly, or that so much water would fall from the sky. The hour and a half of rain was enough to disturb the entire flow of traffic in the city.

My office is on the twentieth floor of an office building. From my window, I can see the Marginal Pinheiros highway below. Sitting in my armchair, I could see the dark clouds move in and cover the sky and darken the entire horizon.

I turned the lights on at the front desk and walked to the pantry to make some coffee. I returned with my mug, resigned to the fact that the possible new patient would never make it to our first session. He would never make it on time, he would get stuck in traffic. Such was life in São Paulo.

Sitting under the office lights I expected at any moment to receive a phone call, the minimum courtesy under the circumstances, canceling the appointment. Meanwhile, so as not to waste time, I began to read the thesis of a student I was advising.

Sergio Y.'s appointment was the last item on my calendar that day, but since he could not make it, I would end my day early. I would stay in the office until the traffic eased up and then I would have an easy commute home.

I would not meet the intelligent and confused young man my college friend had referred to me, but I would have time to read Luciana Cossermelli's thesis, something I needed to do anyway. At that moment, it made no difference whether I met a new patient or finished reading a dissertation on the methodology for establishing public mental health centers. It was all work, and it had to be done.

However, at 5 P.M. on the dot, the office doorbell rang. To my surprise he had arrived on time. I was impressed.

Since the receptionist had left early because of the rain, I opened the door myself. He wore jeans, sneakers and a white T-shirt with a picture of Mickey Mouse. Before greeting me with a handshake, he introduced himself: "I'm Sergio Y. Professor Heloísa Andrade from the Rousseau School referred me. How do you do?"

I recognized the last name and deduced whose son he was. I knew his father by name. At the time, however, I had no way of knowing he owed his straight dark hair to his mother.

In the office, he waited for me to invite him to sit. Then, looking straight at me, very confidently, he took the initiative, and began. He said he had asked the school principal to recommend a therapist because he "wanted to guarantee himself a future that was minimally happy."

"I'm very pessimistic," he said.

He was aware, objectively speaking, that he had everything necessary for a happy life. Good health. Material comforts. Looks. A school he liked. Parents who were good to him.

Despite all of this, he was sad most of the time. Once, he told me: "I'm depressed by nature. I always have been. I can't escape it." Today, in retrospect, it seems clear that it was his refusal to accept this unhappiness that led him to me.

For reasons he could not understand, his mood invariably reverted to a state of unhappiness, which, according to him, seemed a permanent fact of his reality: a sense of constant sorrow, which he could not stop feeling and whose origin he could not identify. His innermost nature was unhappy. The statement "I'm a sad person," just like that, in quotation marks, is in my notes for our first session.

After he left—I remember it well—I needed to clean the office carpet, which his muddy shoes had soiled. While I erased his footprints, I thought that I liked the manner in which he had expressed his thoughts.

In our second session, Sergio Y. asked if he could move to the couch. There, he told me he did not have many friends, but that he did not feel isolated because of this. He spoke of recurring dreams involving his great-grandfather and Armenian ancestors whom he had never heard of and did not even identify with.

His way of expressing himself was unusual for a seventeen-year-old boy. He was loquacious without seeming anxious, and, most importantly, his tone did not irritate me, something that tends to happen with young patients who are referred to me.

It was in our next session that I decided that the case of Sergio Y. in fact interested me. I offered him the Wednesday, 5 to 6 P.M. slot.

He accepted.

THE HAPPINESS THEY PROMISED
AND DID NOT DELIVER

I found Sergio Y.'s most appealing trait to be his integrity. He had all the necessary elements to lead a conventionally happy life. His family, the marketplace and society: everything pointed to a happy life. However, he refused to accept this self-delusion that life suggested to him.

My initial impression was that Sergio Y. tried to maintain a certain autonomy with regard to what family and people who knew him expected. By finding a psychotherapist at seventeen he had shown the courage to challenge the conventional wisdom that for him happiness was unavoidable. He was unhappy and was true to his feelings. For him that was enough.

He had enjoyed good health his entire life. He was 1.87 meters tall and weighed 78 kilos. He did not suffer from any congenital or infectious diseases. He had perfect teeth. Sergio Y. had the physical prerequisites for happiness in abundance.

He had led a sheltered life. Until the age of ten, he had always had a nanny to care for him when he was not in school. His parents were not always available. His father he saw practically only on weekends. His mother he saw sometimes before going to school in the morning and at dinnertime.

He had never seen his parents fight. Sergio's impression was that theirs was a good marriage. He had had a twin brother born with anencephaly who died eight days after birth. Sergio Y.'s only visual memory of his brother was based on a photo he found many years ago, while playing dress-up in his parents' bedroom and going through their wardrobe. There, in one of the drawers, was a photo of a three-day-old baby, eyes closed, face sunken, nestled in his mother's arms, with a cap pulled over his eyebrows to hide his missing skull.

He avoided thinking about that picture. He never opened that drawer again, but he told me he did not believe Roberto's death had anything to do with his sense of unhappiness. He assured me that it did not weigh on him at all.

"My parents made sure I was spared. They never mentioned my brother's death. I never shared in their pain. Had I not found that picture in my mother's wardrobe, I think I'd never have known I'd even had a brother."

In our sessions, he spoke of his parents' expectations and his indecision when it came to his career choice. He considered himself "tough to make friends with." Sometimes he mentioned Sandra, a classmate, for whom he had apparently harbored platonic feelings. He told me he "admired her way of being." When asked if he would like her to be his girlfriend, he said he had "more urgent things to take care of in my life."

I was curious at the mention of "more urgent things," but I wanted him to introduce them spontaneously. I had no clear understanding of what Sergio sought in therapy. I found him mysterious. It seemed better to give it time. So, that is what I decided to do.

Over the course of our sessions, no one theme took precedence. Our therapy was a patchwork quilt. My impression was that, as doctor and patient, we had a nice dynamic, and even a productive one at times, but at the same time an overly slow and cautious one.

One of the recurring themes in our talks was Areg, his great-grandfather, who took the decision to leave Armenia and emigrate to Brazil. Another constant theme was his unhappy condition.

He considered himself unhappy even if it was not readily apparent. He was sober. His grief did not show. If he did not reveal his feelings, no one would have known. No one would have even suspected.

I believe this sobriety was the expression of a soul mature beyond his years. He did not deny his unhappy condition. On the contrary, he recognized it, but he rejected it, he tried to escape it, to defeat it. His seeking therapy was evidence of this. However, he felt no need to publicly display it.

With me he would speak more of his family than of himself. I have the impression that in speaking of his family, he wanted to expose the history from which he came, to show how he fit into a broader narrative. Sergio Y. wanted to make sense of himself, to understand the genealogy of his inescapable unhappiness in order, I hoped, to overcome it.

THE GREAT-GRANDFATHER

The most interesting and productive sessions we had were those where Sergio Y. spoke of his great-grandfather, Areg Yacoubian, who at sixteen boarded a ship for Brazil.

Sergio told me how his great-grandfather had settled in the city of Belém, where a countryman, Hagop Moskofian, had opened a wholesale distribution company four years earlier. His ship arrived in Pará in March of 1915 after making stops in Recife and Fortaleza.

Areg's first job was as a warehouse man. He prided himself on being fast and keeping tight control over inventory. He helped Hagop as needed. For twenty minutes every night before bed, he would struggle to read the news in the *Noticias do Pará* in an attempt to teach himself Portuguese. He had a reputation for being frugal and good-natured and living for his work.

When Areg arrived in Belém, Hagop set him up in a small room above the store, which Areg slowly appropriated during his first year on the job. The space soon became his bedroom—"and his dream room," as Sergio was keen to stress, quoting his great-grandfather.

In 1919, fellow countrymen arriving from Constantinople, fleeing the Turkish massacres, brought news that Areg's family had been deported from Erzerum, where they lived, and had not been seen since. It was later learned that on the same day, in a single blow, Areg lost his entire family—his parents and eleven brothers, who had made the decision not to seek lives happier than those terminated at the hands of Ottoman troops.

According to what Sergio told me—so he had been told—after Areg, the last surviving Yacoubian, learned of his family's death, he never again shed a tear for any reason, either happy or sad.

He knew how to prosper. He became Hagop's partner in the company and, in 1924, at the age of twenty-five, he married Laila, the only daughter of Samir Simon, who owned a women's clothing store in the Comércio district.

Over time, the two Armenians forged a brotherly friendship that lasted a lifetime. They became best friends. Areg continued to be Hagop's partner, but he also opened other businesses by himself or with other partners. He sold everything from toys to industrial ovens. At twelve, his only child, Hagopinho, already worked with him at Laila Stores.

By the time he died at 103, he owned a commercial and real estate empire that practically stretched throughout Brazil.

Areg's importance in forming Sergio Y.'s worldview was immense. This became clear again when, not very long ago, I played back the recording where he told me about his great-grandfather's hundredth birthday party.

I have a recurring dream of my great-grandfather Areg. In the dream, he gives a speech, but I'm the only person in the audience. He begins, but he speaks softly, and I can barely hear him. I move closer, but I can only make out his last word: "happy." I know why I have this dream. It's because of my memories of Areg's hundredth birthday party, in Pará. I went. My whole family traveled to Belém. My parents, my uncle Elias, my aunt Valéria, my cousin José. Everyone. We all stayed in my grandfather Hagopinho's house.

The party was held at my grandparents'. They'd hired a caterer from São Paulo and set up tables on the porch and in the garden. They even set up a tent in case of rain. Between relatives and guests, there were about fifty people. After we all sang "Happy Birthday," Areg called everybody's attention by tapping his wineglass with a fork. When everyone was quiet, he stood. He took out a sheet of paper from his pocket. He held the paper with both hands and stared at it, and it seemed as if he would read from it, but instead he folded the paper and laid it on the table. He cleared his throat and began.

At one hundred, Areg was in good health. He was full of life. He walked slowly but firmly. He spoke softly, but his message always seemed positive. I think most of the guests that evening could not even hear him. But I was close to him, sitting at the family table, and I heard every word. I realized he was choking up and stuttering a bit. I was about eleven or twelve at the time. I remember it all in detail. I've never been able to forget what he said. I think I'm here today because of that day. It was because of his speech that I understood I needed to do something to be happy. I watched Areg's birthday video so often I know the speech by heart. You want to see? I can even do his accent. [. . .]

Once the speech was over, and the guests began greeting him, I walked over and picked up the piece of paper he'd left on the table. I quickly shoved it in my pocket, without thinking, as if I were shoplifting. Later, locked in the bathroom, when I opened the piece of paper, I realized that the only thing Areg had written on it with his shaky handwriting was the words: "If happiness is not where we are, we must chase her. She sometimes lives far away. You must have the courage to be happy."

I brought the sheet of paper with Areg's message to São Paulo. I put it in my datebook in my desk drawer. I have it to this day. It's like a talisman.

THE SPEECH AS HE REMEMBERED IT

Dear friends,

In this celebration of the centennial of my birth, I would first of all like to thank family and friends. I also wish to thank our beloved Brazil, to which I owe everything I have.

I came from a town called Erzerum. There I spent my youth, but there was no joy in living. I could see there was no future. I could feel the war approaching. I needed to get out of there to be happy. Something told me it was my only chance.

Now that I've turned one hundred, I know that life is too short to be sad. A happy life is more happy days than sad ones. So the advice I give to the young ones is this: always try to make your days happy. The important thing is having as many happy days as possible.

We must never forget that sadness exists, because we know sadness really does exist. But you must reject sadness and unhappiness. You must also work hard, because work helps in everything.

When I was a child, I never imagined there was a country on the other side of the world called Brazil—nor that I myself would one day become a Brazilian.

I'm proud I had the courage to leave Armenia to seek my happiness, that I found it, and that I was able to ensure the continuity of my family's name. The family I lost in Erzerum I restarted here in Bélem.

Laila, Hagopinho, Otília, Elias, Valéria, José, Salomão, Tereza and Sergio. My eternal brother, Hagop, who has already left us, who I cannot forget, friends, colleagues. You are the happiness I found in Brazil.

Had I resigned myself and stayed in my city, the place where I was born, our family name would no longer exist. There would be no Areg, there would be no Hagop, there would be no Elias, there would be no Salomão, or Sergio or José. There would be no one. Our name would have disappeared. There would be no Yacoubians here now.

So the message I want to leave the youth is that you must believe in happiness. Then go after her, even if that means you must do something new, that you never could have imagined before. Happiness comes from the courage to do something new. Happiness exists. I am proof of this.

IT WAS WINTER FOR OTHERS, BUT FOR HIM,
IT WAS SUMMER

During the time Sergio worked with me, he suspended treatment just once, for four weks, from December 15, 2006, to January 15, 2007, for vacation.

During those four weeks, Sergio went to New York with his parents. I stayed at my beach house, reading, swimming, taking long walks and supervising the repair of a leak in the guest room which forced me to redo part of the roof.

While I bought cement in Ilhabela, Sergio Y. was reinventing his destiny. I wonder now whether he was still in New York when he decided what he would do with his life, or if it was only later, when he was back in São Paulo and had returned to his daily life.

On one of those days during his vacation, Sergio decided to undertake the most radical journey of his life. I have no way of knowing if he began that journey on a subway ride, the 4 train, or if he arrived at Battery Park by taxi.

But the means of transportation he used to get from his hotel on the Upper East Side to the Immigration Museum on Ellis Island, off the southern tip of Manhattan, where his life began to change, makes no difference. Either way, he would have arrived on the island by ferry. The important thing is that when he stepped off that boat, he was leaving water for firm ground.

In the notes I took and in my recordings of the sessions leading up to that vacation, there are frequent references to New York. I could not imagine in our sessions the importance the city would acquire for Sergio. Since I had lived there once, I suggested some sightseeing options. One of them was a visit to Ellis Island.

"You like stories of courage, so you must go to the museum at Ellis Island. You might find the stories of those immigrants interesting. You'll see their belongings, learn stories about people who, like Areg, bet everything on their own happiness," was more or less what I told him before his trip.

I was aiming at what I saw and hit what I had never seen.

In our first session after the holidays, on the afternoon of January 16, Sergio Y. came to my office a little before his scheduled appointment. In the waiting room, he handed me a plastic bag, one of those duty-free ones. Inside was a small framed print and a hardcover book.

"Sorry, I didn't get the chance to gift wrap it," he said.

The book was an English translation of *The Book of Disquiet* by Fernando Pessoa. The title was superimposed against a purple backdrop. The print was of an old ship elegantly crossing the ocean. A caption read: "SS Kursk, 1910-1936, Barclay, Curle & Co. Ltd. Glasgow, Scotland."

"It's a bilingual edition. I found it helpful. The picture I found on Ellis Island. I hope you like it. It's special. I bought lots of books there. Thanks for the tip," is what he basically said.

I remembered that, at some point, he had told me he liked Fernando Pessoa's poetry. "His concept of heteronyms is amazing. How can one person feel like so many, and in such different ways?" he said during one session.

The fact that he had given me a bilingual edition of his favorite poet was predictable, almost clichéd. I had received exactly the same kind of gift from other patients. It seemed unusual, though, that he should give me a cheap print of a ship called the SS Kursk, which, I later learned, operated between Liepāja and New York at the height of the great European migration to the United States.

I confess that at the time, although grateful for the gesture and the thought, it bothered me a little that Sergio thought I would hang a picture of that quality on my wall. I could see he had bought it at the gift shop of the museum I had recommended. This was how I justified the gift.

For months, I left the SS Kursk picture floating in the office, sometimes on the desk, leaning against a wall, sometimes moored to the books. Now that it has become much more special to me, it is permanently anchored to a spot at the end of the hall, above the shelf. I have positioned it so that it is one of the first objects I see when I arrive at the office.

In his next session, Sergio chose not to lie on the couch. He asked to sit in a chair facing my desk, the same place he had sat the first time he came to see me. Calmly, looking straight into my eyes, he said he no longer wanted to continue his treatment with me. These were his words, sitting in front of me with his car keys in his hand: "Dr. Armando, I think I found a way to be happy. I had a revelation in one of our talks and I think I now know the path I need to follow in my life. I feel like I don't need to come back anymore. I apologize for not saying anything earlier, but I didn't know. Thanks for everything."

That is what he said.

It was as if, after hours and hours of a long bus ride, a passenger were to get up calmly from his seat and, addressing the driver, explain that he had taken the wrong bus and that he needed to get off.

He handed me a check for the sessions he still owed me for, shook my hand and went out into the rain.

The episode put me in a bad mood, and I slept poorly for several days.

I wondered if the process of arriving at this "revelation" he had mentioned could really have been triggered by one of our conversations. If so, which one?

I admired Sergio Y's intelligence. I would have liked to have continued to have him as a patient. His abandoning treatment saddened me greatly as a doctor. But the perfect is the enemy of the good. As a friend of mine liked to say: that's life in the big city. Things do not necessarily happen the way we want them to.

Years later, Sergio Y. no longer occupied my thoughts much, but neither had he completely disappeared from them. In my professional bookkeeping, Sergio Y. was a net capital loss.

Things only began to change one summer afternoon when I went to the shopping center to look at shoes and decided to make a quick stop at the supermarket first.

THE MOTHER'S PERFUME
AND THE SMELL OF CHEESE

I noticed her presence immediately and had the impression she had also noticed mine. We were both waiting for the lone clerk to finish waiting on a lady who was buying buffalo mozzarella.

I wanted to look at her, but instead I decided to turn to the cheeses and avoid that woman, with her black hair pulled back and diamond earrings so big that even I, who am not particularly aware of jewelry, noticed them. Staring at the cheeses, I thought of how obviously she exhibited her wealth. There she was: the female embodiment of a category of people I know very well from my practice.

She asked the clerk for a piece of Parmesan cheese, which she pointed at with her outstretched finger. While waiting for her order, she looked my way, came nearer and spoke:

"Dr. Armando?" she said as if she knew me. "It's Tereza Yacoubian, Sergio's mother. He was a patient of yours a few years back."

At first I didn't understand what she was saying. It took me a couple seconds to retrieve Sergio's name from my memory. I greeted her almost mechanically.

"Nice to meet you, how do you do?"

"I'm fine, thank you," she replied, looking up at me. "I'm sorry for the intrusion, but from the time Sergio was in therapy with you, I've always wanted to tell you something that I've never had the opportunity to say. We have mutual friends, but you know how crazy life in São Paulo can be. We live in the same city, but we might as well live in separate countries."

"That's true," I replied, not knowing what else to say.

I found the whole situation strange, but since Tereza had approached me and was being friendly, I was confident that what she had to say to me would be nice. In fact, at that moment, I was glad that coincidence had put me in touch with the mother of my former patient, who I had not heard from in years.

"You helped my son so much. I don't know how to thank you for all the good you've done Sergio. That's why I took the liberty. You were very good for my son. I wanted to thank you. I didn't want to miss this opportunity. Thank you so much, really."

I did not expect those remarks, and much less that they should end with an expression of gratitude. It made me blush, but I liked hearing it.

"I thank you, Tereza. I'm glad to know I was able to help. Sergio is a very intelligent boy. How is he doing? What is he doing?" I asked, trying to be friendly.

"He's happy. He moved to New York a month after he stopped his treatment with you. He's been living there ever since. It's been almost four years. He's changed completely. If you ran into him, you wouldn't recognize him. He graduated from culinary school in June. He's crazy about cooking. This cheese I'm buying is for a recipe he sent me. His father is opening a little restaurant for him so he can gain experience. It's tiny, only eight tables. Earlier today, he called to tell me he finally got his liquor license . . . "

"He's opened a restaurant? What a surprise! Does it have a name yet?"

"Yes, it's called Angelus," she said.

"Angelus? That's different . . . Is it in Manhattan?"

"Yes. On Hudson Street, almost at the corner of Charles. Do you know where that is?"

"More or less. It's in the West Village, right?"

"That's right."

"Then I know where it is. So, Sergio is okay and happy?"

"He's doing great. I don't think he could be any better. And a lot of that happiness he owes to you. As a mother, I also owe a lot to you. I only hope I can repay you some day."

"Please send him my regards. I have a daughter doing her MBA in New York. She's graduating next year. Tell him when I go to her graduation ceremony, I'll pay a visit to his restaurant." The clerk had Tereza's order ready and was patiently waiting for our conversation to end.

"I'll tell him. I'm sure he'll love to know that I ran into you in the supermarket."

We parted ways with a hesitant handshake that evolved into a kiss on the cheek.

I asked the clerk for two hundred grams of curd cheese. While he removed the cheese from the window, I basked in the good news I had just received regarding Sergio and his restaurant.

Sergio's father was a well-known businessman. He ran a family chain of appliance stores with locations throughout Brazil. Sergio could live well wherever he pleased, and he could choose to do whatever he wanted. But, as the only son of Salomão Yacoubian, one might expect him to be living in São Paulo, fulfilling his destiny in the family business.

Apparently, due to life's vagaries, he had not yet fulfilled that destiny. He had studied cooking and was about to open a restaurant in New York, all with his parents' support. Who could have foreseen this? I for one would never have guessed it. I was surprised. Learning about his situation and his progress was by far the best news I had heard that day.

Sergio might become famous one day. He would appear in magazines and documentaries. People would make reservations three months in advance to sit at one of the few tables in his restaurant in the West Village.

I think this is what I wanted for him.

He could, however, turn into yet another failed little rich boy, whose life went nowhere. The restaurant could fail, he could change his mind, he could open another business and it too could fail. Laila Shops would give him a business card and an allowance, and that would be that. He would go on with his life without major consequences for him or anyone else.

During therapy, his interest in the culinary arts never came up. For me, the image of Sergio as a chef, a restaurant owner, was almost an implausible one, one which I would have to get used to. But the truth was that I did not have enough information to judge his decision. What I had were impressions. I could not gauge the strength of his will.

However, regardless of his reasons for doing so, it was clear Sergio had decided to take his destiny into his own hands. At least for now, he would not be selling stoves, would not be filling the role of presumptive heir to a chain of stores where thousands of Brazilians bought their flat-screen televisions in forty-eight installments.

For this, it seems, he needed to leave São Paulo. At least for a while. He had charted his own life strategy, which now he was living out. Apparently, he was happy.

Even if partially so, Sergio's happiness had been credited to me by his own mother. What I felt at that moment was a sense of pride and satisfaction.

Nearly four years after our last session, that was all I knew about him. Right then and there, in my mind, I discharged Sergio Y. He entered my huge gallery of satisfied clients.

Finally, I could forget him.

The meeting with Tereza Yacoubian had cheered me up. I felt gratified. What is more, I even liked her perfume. I left the supermarket and, in a spirit of general satisfaction, I went to a shoe store and bought some moccasins I had been eyeing, but that had seemed too expensive before I had met the mother of my satisfied patient.

OBSESSION, DEATH, BURIAL AND TRANSFORMATION

I am a bit of a germaphobe. I say "a bit" because I believe my obsession is under control. I have my preferences and my way of doing things, but they do not result in mental blocks which prevent me from leading a normal life. If I were to wash my hands every time I had the urge, I would do it about thirty times a day. However, if needed, I can go a whole day without washing them, although it might cause me great consternation.

About six or seven years ago I came to the conclusion that newsprint made my hands dirty. This caused me such discomfort that at a certain point I simply decided to stop reading newspapers altogether so as not to dirty my fingers. One day, someone told me about Japanese gloves made for this exact purpose: handling newspaper without staining one's fingers. I found them in a store in Liberdade and I bought twelve packets all at once. They cost me an arm and a leg, but for many years they gave me peace of mind while reading.

Now things are different. I read the news online. I spray an antiseptic solution once every night on my computer keyboard just to satisfy my obsessional neurosis. I also use a mini vacuum cleaner and a hand sanitizer. With these measures I manage.

Every day, between midnight and one A.M., after reviewing my day's notes, I turn on my computer. First, I check my e-mail. I reply to those messages that require immediate attention. Then, I proceed to the others. When I have answered everything I can, usually at about 1:30 A.M., I start reading the online newspapers.

Sometimes, depending on when I go to bed, I can read the next day's edition. When this happens, I have the advantage of waking up having already read the day's news. The downside is that, during the day, the news rarely surprises me because I have already read it. But at least it frees up time for other activities.

My early morning reading sessions help me relax. The light from the screen hypnotizes me after a while. Slowly, I begin to doze off. I'm not the only one who uses reading to induce sleep. A lot of people do. Around 2 to 2:15 A.M., I turn off the computer, get up, brush my teeth and go to bed.

The problem is that some news is so disturbing that instead of inducing sleep, it causes restlessness and anxiety.

The first time a news story struck me as so disconcerting that I could not sleep was in 2001, on September 11. The detailed coverage of the attacks on New York disturbed me deeply. Today, the memory of all that destruction has dissipated. But I think I will never forget what I felt then. I spent the night awake, turning over images and thoughts in my mind that I could not digest.

The second time I felt something similar, that kept me completely awake, was about a year ago, in February of 2011. I was about to turn off the computer when I came across the following item:

New York police have identified the body found on Thursday as that of Sergio Yacoubian, the son of businessman Salomão Yacoubian. Yacoubian, 23, lived in Manhattan, where he owned a restaurant. The Brazilian fell from the fourth floor of his home in the West Village. Police believe he may have been the victim of a homicide, although there are no suspects yet. When contacted by this reporter in São Paulo, the family refused comment.

Perhaps some unconscious defense mechanism was at work, but I did not associate the victim with my former patient right away. The name seemed familiar, but I needed a few seconds to make the connection between that dead Brazilian in Manhattan and the Sergio Y whom I had only really discharged from my care a few weeks ago.

The news astonished me. My initial reaction was one of denial. I hoped to discover that it was a namesake, of the same age and same profession. He had been my patient. His mother had told me he was fine. He had everything he needed to be happy. He was young. It could not be him.

But it was.

In general, learning that someone of an advanced age has died does not move me. As a doctor, I am very familiar with the fact that age degenerates and kills the body. For me, it is clear that life leads to death. For me, it is easy to accept.

An old man has had time to experience life's defining moments. The death of a man who has had time to live should arouse no pity. It is not that I do not regret the loss of that person, but the death of an elderly individual does not affect me very deeply. Everyone dies, really. It is just a matter of who goes first.

On the other hand, I have a hard time assimilating the death of a young person. It moves me to hear when their lives have been cut short. They die of incurable diseases, needless traffic accidents, in a climate of outrage. Even when peaceful, their deaths are always violent.

Not only do the young die prematurely; they also die in fear. And to die young and in fear is the worst way to die, because death looks the victim in the eye and it is recognized. The victim has time to see death coming and to understand that he is about to die.

The body of the fearful boy found in the backyard of his home in Manhattan and the body of my former patient coincided in name, nationality and DNA. They lived in the same city. They were the same age. There were no dissimilarities.

On the Internet, I tried researching the crime in the New York newspapers but to no avail. The death merited a small note in an unimportant newspaper. It was the only record.

Sergio Y., twenty-three-year-old, Brazilian, a culinary school graduate, perhaps a promising restaurant owner, a former patient of Dr. Armando's, was murdered in Manhattan.

My teenage patient, Salomão Yacoubian's sole heir, moves to New York to study cooking and ends up dead, at whose hands and why, nobody knows. For all practical purposes, this was the chain of events I first formed in my mind.

Then came the questions. What happened? Did he get involved in drugs? Who killed him? A friend? A burglar? A girlfriend? An employee? How did a patient who had left my office full of optimism get to this point? What were the events leading up to his foreign death?

There were no answers, Sergio's death made no sense to me. I could think of nothing else. The circumstances surrounding his death became my obsession.

The truth is that I knew very little. I did not have enough elements to satisfactorily answer the questions I had about the murder. I knew that death had been inflicted, that it had not been natural. I could deduce nothing further, I could only imagine.

In the days that followed, I looked for information about Sergio Y.'s death in the press but found nothing.

Four days after reading the news that had kept me awake all night, I found the following funeral notice, which was published in the two leading newspapers of São Paulo:

It is with great sadness that Tereza and Salomão Yacoubian fulfill the duty of communicating the death of their son SERGIO EMÍLIO YACOUBIAN, which occurred on February 2nd in

New York City. Mass for the benefit of his soul will be held on February 9, at 11 A.M., at the Armenian Apostolic Church of Brazil, on Avenida Santos Dumont, 55, in the city of São Paulo.

I have since learned that, while I agonized over unanswered questions, Tereza and Salomão had gone to New York, accompanied by their lawyer, in order to release their son's body.

The New York City Police Department took five days to authorize sending the body to Brazil. The coffin went straight from the airport to the cemetery, where only the closest relatives attended the funeral. Once underground, Sergio Y. could finally disappear, yielding his place in the world to someone else.

I chose a very dark charcoal suit for the Mass. I put on a white dress shirt and a purple tie, the color of mourning, to convey an air of solemnity, in my view appropriate when in the physical presence of death. The day was sunny, and I wore sunglasses. I sat in one of the last pews, my mind devoid of thoughts, waiting, listening to the priest recite the liturgy, taking my cue from the others when to stand and sit.

Only once during Mass did my gaze cross paths with Tereza's. She looked me straight in the eyes, quickly but deeply, for two seconds. Then she unlocked her eyes and stared off into infinity. At Mass, Tereza could see no one. There, the good I had done for Sergio Y. no longer mattered.

When Mass was over, before leaving, I went to the front of the altar to offer my condolences.

"Thank you for coming," she said without looking up.

"I wouldn't have missed it. I liked him very much," I replied.

She took my right hand with both her hands. She shook her head sadly, always with her eyes downcast. I reached out to shake Salomão's hand, and he greeted me formally, not quite sure who I was.

Before leaving the church, I felt an urgent need to wash my hands. At the sink in the bathroom next to the sacristy, with soapy hands, I had a near-hallucinatory event. Suddenly I had the impression that my hands were stained with blood. I felt blood on my palms, nails, and in between my fingers. Under the tap water, with plenty of soap, I slowly managed to remove that imaginary blood.

It was shortly after that I started having frequent nightmares, involving the various doubts that remained in my mind surrounding Sergio Y.'s death.

From the people I talked to—two friends of the family, who were also acquaintances of mine—I learned very little. I was unable to even learn the general circumstances surrounding what had happened. The only thing I knew was that he had been murdered. I still had no idea who the perpetrator had been or the reasons.

I thought about calling Tereza. I could perhaps extract from her information that would help satisfy the tremendous curiosity I felt concerning her son's death, one that was beginning to trouble me.

Despite my desire to call, I did not. I could not be so brazen. I did not regret it. At the time, I did what seemed right, but the fact is I remained totally in the dark, knowing nothing about Sergio Y.'s murder.

My curiosity turned into an obsession. I spent hours on end creating different scenarios in my mind surrounding my former patient's death. I dreamed of possible murderers, Sergio's falling body, his terrified face, dressed as a chef, his head bleeding, covered in snow in the backyard of his home.

I began waking up in the middle of the night and lost my appetite completely. Two weeks after these symptoms began, an idea occurred to me as to how I might obtain answers to my most basic questions surrounding the case. My reasoning went as follows:

Sergio had been murdered in his home in the West Village. According to the article in the newspaper, Manhattan police had opened an investigation into the murder. Therefore, the answers I sought I would find in the outcome of their investigations.

Perhaps the police already knew the circumstances surrounding Sergio Y.'s murder. Who had killed him, and why. If the investigation had been completed, I might at least gain access to some of the answers.

The records of the alleged murder must reside somewhere in the Manhattan court system. If a suspect had been arraigned, there would also exist information concerning the court case. With any luck, there would even be transcripts of witness depositions. My curiosity about the circumstances surrounding the death of Sergio Y. would be satisfied in the New York courts.

The next day, while showering, after returning from the gym, something I already knew but had not thought of occurred to me: in the United States, information regarding court proceedings are public records. Therefore, anyone who files a formal request, even through a lawyer, can access information on any crime committed in the country.

I asked a cousin—the son of my aunt Yeda, with whom my mother had lived on Jauaperi Street—who works as a lawyer, if he knew a firm in the US that could help me obtain information about a homicide that had occurred in Manhattan.

"I'll talk to our office in New York to see how we can do this. The crime was committed in Manhattan, right?" was the only question he asked me.

Two days after our conversation, my cousin called. He had spoken to the New York firm, and they recommended a private investigation agency, which could navigate the intricacies of the police bureaucracy and identify and select relevant information of interest to me in the case. The American lawyer with whom my cousin had spoken offered to request the information from the agency.

"It'll set you back about two thousand dollars, but at least you'll have no worries, and they'll send you copies of all the files, everything aboveboard, I think it's worth it. Here's the e-mail of the guy in New York. Write to him, he's waiting for you to contact him," my cousin Jorge said.

Later that same day, I wrote to Oliver Hoskings. I asked for information concerning the possible murder of a Brazilian citizen, Sergio Y., on February 2, 2010, in the West Village.

I received an answer to my email about fifteen minutes later. Hoskings asked me to confirm the full name of the victim and that the death had occurred in the borough of Manhattan. I wrote to him confirming the information, and he promised to be in touch shortly.

Three days later, I received a message from Oliver Hoskings stating that there was no record of a murder or an attempted murder of a Sergio Emílio Y. in Manhattan on the date indicated. He asked if I would like to broaden the search to three days before and three days after February 2nd, which I agreed to.

He wrote to me again the next day. He said he could assure me that there was no death certificate for a Sergio Y. in Manhattan. However, he called my attention to a strange fact: another person with that same last name had been murdered on Grove Street in the West Village, on the day I had initially specified. He asked if I wanted information on that other individual. I was intrigued by the coincidence and said yes.

Of all the information that Hoskings forwarded me, the only facts that did not make sense were the first name (Sandra) and the sex (female) of the murder victim on Grove Street, on February 2, 2010. My American lawyer had managed to piece together a narrative from his search of the court records.

The body of Sandra Yacoubian was found facedown in a

pool of her own blood by Edna Alves, a Brazilian maid. Ms. Yacoubian, born in São Paulo, Brazil, on January 10, 1988, was pushed from a fourth-floor window by a neighbor. She fell, broke her neck and bled to death in the backyard of the house she shared with her assassin at 12 Grove Street.

Shortly before her death, Sandra had been drinking, and there was evidence that she had been smoking marijuana too. She had been pushed out the window by the downstairs neighbor. The townhouse they had shared had been advertised in the market as "magnificent." Sandra's apartment occupied the top two floors. Laurie Clay, her murderer, occupied the bottom two.

Like Sandra, Ms. Clay was twenty-three years old. She studied fashion at New York University and wrote a style blog on the Internet. Her family came from Louisville, Kentucky, and she was the heiress of the largest mustard producer in the state. She surrendered voluntarily to police, five days after the crime.

Laurie claimed she had been under the influence of drugs and alcohol when she killed Sandra. That she had been ordered do to so by God, who had appeared to her in a hallucination. She was sentenced to twenty-two years in prison and was incarcerated at the Beacon Correctional Facility in the town of Beacon, about 100 kilometers north of New York.

At Hoskings's suggestion, a search was done to determine whether there was in the civil records of New York anything indicating that Sergio Emílio Y. had, at some point, changed his identity.

That is how I discovered that Sergio Y. and Sandra Yacoubian were the same person. Or rather, that they were distinct branches of the same body. Sergio, who had acquired American citizenship thanks to an investor visa, formally filed a request in August 2009 to change his name and gender in a Manhattan court, which recognized the request and authorized the change. The grounds given for the request was "transsexuality."

After I discovered and understood what had happened to Sergio Y., I went into shock. It was as if I had fallen ill. To this day, I still do not understand exactly what happened to me. I became apathetic. I could not concentrate. I stopped eating. I lost almost six kilos in one month.

As bedtime approached, I felt an unease, a discomfort that I only managed to free myself from with a warm bath and some antianxiety medication. Sometimes I would sleep well at night and wake up in a relaxed mood. Other times, however, I would spend all night awake, unable to sleep until daybreak.

I felt obliged to review all my notes and to listen to all my recordings of Sergio's sessions. Our years of analysis had yielded a green-covered notebook and multiple computer files.

I spent a whole afternoon reviewing my notes. Often they seemed disjointed. After five years, our memory fades and becomes selective. I had to accept that many of the words and conclusions I had jotted down concerning Sergio no longer made sense to me. I could not even remember what they referred to. Only sentence fragments and underlined words remained. Nowhere in the notebook was there any mention of "transsexual" or "transsexuality," which was lamentable for a doctor of the caliber I judged myself to be.

Based on what I could ascertain from reviewing my notes, Sergio Y. felt unhappy and did not want to resign himself to the unhappy condition he had found himself in. Once he had told me that he was "the fruit of my great-grandfather's courage." If Areg had stayed where he had been born, he would have died, have been murdered, and he, Sergio, would never have been born. "Abandoned where he'd lived to continue living." I wrote that sentence down in quotation marks. I think even then, Sergio Y. saw immigration as a way to ensure his survival and his future.

Surprisingly, mention of New York jumped out in these notes. "New York as a possibility for reinvention" (08/08/2006), written in blue ink. "Trip to New York, on vacation. Visit to the Ellis Island Museum"(11/12/2006), in black ink. It became clear to me that, somehow, Sergio's future in New York was already recorded in these notes.

When I had questions or wanted to deepen or clarify something I came across in my notebooks, I would listen to the recording for the corresponding session. It was strange to hear his voice knowing he was dead. The sensation I had when I went back to the recordings was that he was speaking from beyond, using the computer as a speaker. That week, I spent two afternoons and two nights listening to the dead Sergio Y. discuss his life.

IT IS ALL MY FAULT

I never saw any evidence that Sergio Y. was a transsexual. Neither did he ever mention anything that would, in my opinion, indicate an inner conflict over his sexual identity. It seems incredible, but I did not notice anything.

When Tereza Yacoubian approached me in front of the cheese counter at the supermarket and told me her son lived in New York, I found it perfectly natural. I could imagine him living in New York. It made sense. It seemed plausible.

However, it was difficult to reconcile what I thought I knew about Sergio with the discoveries I was now making with regards to his condition as a transsexual and the circumstances surrounding his premature death.

For me, the questions were now different: What role might I have had in the tragic fate of Sergio Y.? Was I as important as I deemed myself to be when I heard he was happy?

When his mother told me he was fine in New York and opening a restaurant in the West Village at twenty-three, I felt responsible for his happiness. I felt I had helped construct his happy life or at least been a catalyst. I even bought a pair of moccasins I had been flirting with as a reward.

Whose responsibility was it now that my patient's happy life was over? Was that mine too? Was I guilty of not acting? Was I guilty of not seeing? Of malpractice? Negligence? Arrogance?

But even if I were guilty, no one but me would ever know. The Federal Medical Council could not revoke my license. They would not even open an investigation. They would never make the connection between Sergio Y.'s death and our therapy sessions. Sergio died years later, in the United States, the victim of another crime.

But what did I say that led him to the tragic circumstances that precipitated his demise? How could I not have noticed his greatest affliction? Did I somehow help him arrive at the warped revelation that led to his death? According to Sergio himself, it was a conversation we had had that led him to his "revelation" as to what he should do with his life.

And what did he do with his life? He disfigured it. He surrendered it to a murderer.

I went to the cemetery twice to visit his grave. "Sergio Emílio Yacoubian, 01/10/1988 - 02/02/2011" is written on the gravestone. Sandra did not leave a record of her brief life on that tombstone. Sandra was born Sergio and remained Sergio in death.

After Sergio's death, my work with patients became less enjoyable. What had once felt stimulating now felt threatening. I began to imagine a different death for each one of my patients, one caused by me. My patients were no longer proof of the good work I was doing but instead began to represent the possibility of error. My shortcomings could mean the death of each one of them, as apparently had already happened once.

At that moment, all I wanted was to wash off the blood I could not help feeling was on my hands. When patients canceled, I now felt relief. I expended too much energy in every session and paid too high a price in terms of the discomfort I felt. Just being around patients became torture. I had to rid myself of these feelings. I did not bother with excuses. "We need to suspend treatment for three weeks." I went on vacation.

I felt I was not coping with the psychological anguish and guilt which Sergio's death had triggered in me. Before the problem grew any worse and made me seriously ill, I decided to talk to Eduardo, a friend from my university days, whom I have known for over forty years.

Eduardo is the person I discuss my cases with. I talk to him when I have doubts and want a second opinion. We talked twice before I left on vacation. But my consternation with regard to my patients persisted.

During the three weeks I was away, I spent only four nights at the beach house, just to make sure things were all right. The rest of the time I stayed in São Paulo. I would go to the gym in the mornings, and to the cinema at night, for at that time the International Film Festival was on.

On the one hand, I tried to be as productive with my time as possible. On the other, I wanted to be transported as far away from my everyday existence as possible. I wanted to escape the present. Today I see things more clearly. At the time, I was not sure if I knew what was going on.

The main source of my frustration was not having detected any hint of Sergio Y.'s transsexuality. I felt I had been duped solely and exclusively by my own incompetence. I had always thought that the secret to transsexuality was not all that deep, that it revealed itself in all of the individual's attitudes, at all times, in all the decisions he or she took, since early childhood. As far as I was concerned, the pain in the patient's soul and their inner confusion would be so visible that one did not need to be a Freudian or Jungian psychoanalyst to make the diagnosis.

Medical malpractice. Not so different from a doctor who fails to diagnose meningitis. I remember a professor of mine in medical school, Dr. Pedro Veríssimo, who liked to say, "Malpractice can always be avoided." I had failed at my job and felt that my incompetence was the key element in the tragedy that led to Sergio Y.'s death.

But he never mentioned anything that I could have interpreted as indicating any conflict over his sexual identity. Not once. I have no idea how many layers of fear drowned out this secret inside of him. It was all hidden. He, of course, knew what was happening and willingly said nothing. He did not have the obligation to tell me anything. We must respect the patient's will.

Eduardo did not seem shocked at my professional failure. One of the first comments he made after I told him of my anguish was, "I don't know why you care so much about a case that's unsolvable. Death really has no solution, Armando. All of these therapies we do only have meaning while we're alive. The dead are useless to us. Sergio Y. died, right? Things are not so black-and-white. This obvious fact is what I want to impress upon you. The responsibility you feel you have in the case of Sergio Y. is unfounded, almost ridiculous. Wake up, Armando! You're merely one of the many factors in the equation that resulted in the death of this twenty-three-year-old. You weren't the determining factor here. You have no idea under what circumstances his death occurred. The sad truth, Armando, is that in this case, your role was minimal. I know you. I know it's hard for you to accept a minor role, but I think that's what you need to try to do."

At the time I did not understand that I had inadvertently reproduced in my mind the stereotype that the death of a transsexual is always caused by the tragic circumstances of his life.

But the death of Sergio Y.—regardless of whether he was a transsexual or not—might have been random. His life might not have been tragic at all. This also happens. That was the conclusion I should try to reach. If he had been hit by a stray bullet, or lightning, or a runaway car in São Paulo or in New York, he would be just as dead. Still young, transsexual and dead, regardless of the agent of his death.

With this psychological guidance in mind, I went on with my life. Gradually, I went back to seeing my regular patients and to going to the gym in the mornings. I felt at peace, but I still thought daily of the nature of my role in the untimely death of my former patient.

Time, however, wears everything down, and gradually the feelings of responsibility for having harmed Sergio Y. began to dissipate. The more I managed to distance myself from the problem, the more my guilt began to turn into doubt.

Reviewing my datebook, I see that I decided to call Tereza on March 19.

It was raining heavily. From my window, I could see the headlights reflected on the wet highway below. The sound of rain drowned out the hum of the traffic. The soaked and tense city grew dark. That afternoon, the main concern of the inhabitants of São Paulo was to get home.

My Thursday patient called at 5:20 P.M. telling me he would not be arriving on time for his session. His call gave me thirty free minutes before my next meeting—a student who wanted my opinion about a project, but who might also not make it because of the rain.

I decided to take advantage of the additional time to answer e-mails and to pay my credit card statement online. From my bank page, I started surfing the web aimlessly, until, don't ask me how, I arrived at the Brazilian Oncology Association page.

I only mention my wanderings on the computer because that was how I arrived at photos of the National Cancer Institute anniversary dinner. The third picture showed Tereza and Salomão Yacoubian with the president of the institute. Salomão wore a dark blue suit, white shirt and burgundy tie; his wife wore a gray dress and looked directly at the camera. It was not a look of celebration, but they hid their sorrow with dignity.

That afternoon, on impulse, I called Tereza Yacoubian. It crossed my mind that this call could be seen as inappropriate, but I decided to interpret the fact that they had been photographed at a social event as evidence that their mourning had come to an end. I chose to believe that photo meant they were accessible.

That was what I was thinking when I picked up the telephone to call.

"Tereza? How are you? This is Armando, I was Sergio's therapist. Do you have a moment? I'm sorry to call you like this, out of the blue. But I've been reviewing my notes from our sessions and I had some questions I wanted to ask you, if you don't mind. I've had dreams of Sergio. In my dream, he wore an apron. I think it's the image you gave me when we met in supermarket."

"I was buying cheese for a soufflé . . . "

"How did this happen, Tereza? What happened to Sergio?"

"Doctor, we still don't understand fully. I can't speak about this just yet. It's not that I don't want to. I'd like to talk to you about Sergio. Just like you have questions for me, I also have questions for you. It's just that I can't now. I'm afraid I'll fall apart. You know how important you were in the decisions he made. If you have questions of a medical nature, I can give you his doctor's e-mail in New York. If you like, I can write to her and say you'll be in touch. Her name is Cecilia Coutts. She can explain what happened to Sergio. But as I said, it's still too painful to talk about my son's death. Please write down Dr. Coutts's e-mail."

"Of course, Tereza. Please excuse the call," I said.

I wrote down the address she gave me. "As soon as I'm able to, we'll talk," she said before hanging up.

I felt embarrassed by the call. At that moment, I felt sorry that I had given in to my impulse.

I had attempted to satisfy my curiosity without regard for the feelings of a mother who had lost her only son. I felt awful. How much lower could I go? I wanted her to understand that what seemed like mere curiosity on my part was not curiosity at all but concern. When someone shows concern for a child who has died, he gives comfort to the surviving parents because that interest is noble and resuscitating.

"Doctor Armando, I appreciate your interest in my son, but I can't help you now. I'll help when I feel up to it."

Suddenly, I realized that for Tereza, Sergio was still unburied.

I would stay up until late reading the news online. I would wake up at around 8 A.M. I would make coffee and feed the cat. I would see the patients I had to see, I would return phone calls, and through it all life apparently remained the same.

The only conspicuous change in my routine was the absence of my cleaning lady, Rosa, who was on maternity leave. Her cousin Rosangela came instead. The presence of one made up for the absence of the other. Nonetheless, in the months that followed Sergio Y.'s death, much had changed for me. I had become cowardly and less committed as a doctor. The death of Sergio Y. had made me a worse person.

A sense of guilt began to weigh on me, and a sadness, which I did not want anyone to know, filled my heart. I did not feel diminished, but I was filled with shame.

Sergio had been the great failure of my professional life. I believed I had never been so wrong with a patient as I was with him. It was only fair that my hands should feel dirty with a blood so real I could almost smell it. But I did not want anyone to know how vulnerable I was.

The only person who knew was Eduardo, my friend from college, who was discreet by nature and always sensible in his advice. He understood how I felt without ever blaming me in any way.

THE THINGS WE DO FOR LOVE

Mariana was born on the eve of my forty-fourth birthday. By then I already had white hair and a belly. I never expected to have children. It was a surprise when Heloísa told me she was pregnant.

Even nowadays it is hard to understand the transformation that occurs when a child is born. One's worldview changes. Old worries fade; others, new ones, emerge. Important things become trivial. This is true even with cats and dogs.

I would not say I was an absent father, but I know I sacrificed time I could have spent with my daughter. I do not regret it. With the time I sacrificed, I did important things for other people. After Heloísa's death Mariana and I became closer. It was a silver lining.

My daughter is beautiful and polite. She has always been a good student. As a sophomore in college she interned at a German bank on Avenida Paulista. She was in her third year studying economics when her mother died. She was twenty.

Shortly before graduating, she told me she wanted to continue her studies. She had decided she wanted to do her MBA in the United States. She did everything herself. She filled out the applications. Wrote her essays. Obtained her letters of recommendation.

She devoted months to the effort. But it was worth it. She was accepted everywhere she had applied to. She chose Columbia University because she would have the opportunity to live in New York. I supported her choice. She asked me to help her financially, and I did.

One of the good memories I have was when I helped her move into her dormitory. She would live in a room about twenty-five square meters in size, with a small kitchen and bathroom.

We bought a bed, a desk and some other furniture from a store the university recommended. The two of us assembled the furniture ourselves. For those few days, we spent hours together, talking as friends. I returned to São Paulo proud. I liked knowing she was a student at one of the best universities in the world. I thought she would be able to build a good life for herself and do interesting things. It gave me a feeling of well-being knowing I had fulfilled my paternal duties alone.

Sergio Y. died on February 2. Four months and six days later, on June 8, Mariana's graduation ceremony would take place.

Prior to Sergio's death, I was looking forward to my trip to New York. After learning of his death, though, the trip became a sacrifice, something I would have to do for love, not pleasure. But I could not miss the graduation.

I had a special relationship with New York. Like my daughter, I went to school there. It was where I discovered what I wanted to do with my life. It was there that I decided to become a psychiatrist.

Soon after graduating, on the advice of a teacher at the Universidade de São Paulo, I applied for a residency at Mount Sinai in New York. At the time, it was very rare for them to accept foreigners. To the surprise of some (but not all), they accepted me.

I arrived on August 4, 1973, on a PanAm flight. It was the first time I had traveled outside of Brazil. Soon after my arrival, with the help of the hospital staff, I found a little one-bedroom on 102nd Street, near the East River. The rental was on the fourth floor of a dilapidated building, with no elevator—one of those with the fire escape outside the window—where several other medical residents lived.

I took my job seriously. I had always studied hard, but during my residency I studied like never before. Most of my days were spent locked in the hospital, breathing air-conditioned air, exposed to sterile light, absorbing all the information I could, with a medical book always at my side in case a free moment should arise.

On Sundays, I would take a break from diagnosing disease and discussing community psychotherapy techniques, and I would go on long walks around the city. I could have gone with one of my fellow residents, but I preferred going alone, to avoid having to make concessions. I wanted to conquer the city in my own way. I did not want to share it with anyone else.

I have wonderful memories of those times and those walks. I would spend all day walking, consulting maps in search of places I wanted to visit, or just wandering aimlessly, feeling the city move around me.

After I returned to São Paulo, whenever I got the chance, I would go back to New York. On those trips back, I would do my best to recreate the same sense of possibility and confidence in the future that had filled me when I was a resident there, when I thought I could do and be anything in life. After all, I thought at the time, how many Brazilian doctors, fresh out of college, get accepted as residents at one of the best hospitals in the world?

I would walk the city streets looking up, arching my head back, unable to see the tops of buildings, believing that my possibilities, and the New York buildings, reached out to infinity. It was this sense of renewal that over the years I sought to replicate in my random walks through Manhattan.

Here, now, sitting in my office, I close my eyes and imagine the sun's rays piercing through the buildings at 9 A.M. to form pools of light on the sidewalk on Third Avenue. I can smell the detergent and fabric softener wafting onto passersby from the 98th Street Laundromat.

After I learned of Sergio's death, my relationship with New York changed. The idea of being in the same city where he had died began to disturb me. It would mean thinking much more of him and his death than I would have liked. What is more, as a doctor I would feel the obligation to visit Dr. Cecilia Coutts, to gain more information about the Sergio-Sandra case, a case I had so obviously misdiagnosed.

New York, the city for which I had harbored only positive feelings and gratitude, had now also become the scene of the death of Sergio Y. To visit it would mean facing my own guilt.

Since the trip could not be avoided, I tried convincing myself that the sacrifice I was making was voluntary and insignificant when compared to the consequences my igno-rance could have caused. Besides, there was also Mariana, whom I could not disappoint. With this in mind, I decided to ignore my fears. I bought my ticket and booked a hotel on 57th Street. I would be in town for four nights. I would arrive on Monday and leave Friday.

I would visit the places Sergio had been: the school where he had studied, the street where he had lived, the store where he bought cooking utensils. At any moment I could be step-ping into the footprints he had left on his journey through New York.

It would be a way to find him once again. We would be like two actors filmed against the same backdrop at different times. We would find each other in space, but be lost to each other in time. Sergio Y. and I would recognize each other in the land-scape of New York.

NEW YORK

In college I had convinced myself that Eduardo was one of the most sensible people in the world. I still hold this view today. Was this because of the opinions and advice I have received over the years? I could not say exactly.

In our conversations about my performance in the Sergio Y. case, he was always emphatic that I should look up Sergio's doctor in New York, Dr. Cecilia Coutts. I still had the e-mail address Tereza gave me when I called her on that rainy afternoon when I had been stood up by one of my patients.

It was Eduardo's arguments, more than anything else, that made clear to me my professional obligation to contact Dr. Coutts. I delayed it for as long as I could. Three days before my departure, however, I wrote her an e-mail introducing myself and asking if, during my brief stay in New York, she would be available for a quick chat about a former patient of ours.

By seeking her out, I was taking a step toward fulfilling my duty as a professional. Deep down, however, I hoped the short notice would prevent any possible meeting between the two of us from ever taking place.

Nonetheless, the next morning, in response to my query, I found the following message from Cecilia Coutts in my inbox:

> Dear Dr. Armando,
> I would be glad to meet you for coffee. Can you come to my office this coming Thursday, at 10 A.M.?

Best regards, C. Coutts, MD, PhD
73 Barrow Street, NY, NY 10014

The friendly tone intrigued me. What kind of woman was she? A doctor who specialized in transgender patients with the surname of an English banker. We agreed to meet on the afternoon of June 9th, on the eve of my return to Brazil.

I did not know it at the time, but the trip would offer me many lessons in humility: the realization that I was not as smart as I thought; the confirmation that I knew very little about Sergio Y. and that I had horribly underestimated him; the realization that the city was still there, but that the building where I lived on 102nd Street had been demolished and no longer existed. The realization that my daughter was an adult and no longer needed me. All of it, even when positive, was humiliating.

I would go to New York for my daughter's sake and I would take the opportunity to learn more about a case that I had not known how to treat. Naively, I thought that knowing more about Sergio Y. would help me reduce the risk of bringing about a similar tragic fate to my other patients. By expanding my medical knowledge I could become a better human being. I thought that was the way out: the doctor in me had to save the person in me.

I confess my conversations with Eduardo had not fully redeemed me. I still carried feelings of guilt that were hard to shake. But I knew that in order to overcome this problem, I would have to transform my feelings regarding Sergio's death into simple curiosity regarding the disappearance of someone I once knew. Self-preservation demanded I accept Sergio's fate indifferently, as though there had never been anything between us.

In the days leading up to the trip, I was anxious. As the plane prepared for takeoff, I was filled with a mix of excitement and anxiety. I closed my eyes and breathed deeply, trying to relax. I saw Sergio, on his back, in a brick yard covered in snow; I saw blood coming out of his head and staining platinum-blond hair I had never seen; I could see red lipstick smudged on Sergio's dead face. I could see the cooking school where he had studied with French chefs with mustaches and aprons covered in sheep's blood.

I took an anxiolytic to relieve the stress. I removed my shoes, reclined my seat and put in earplugs. I began reading a magazine. I slept right through breakfast. I woke up, dazed, to the announcement that we were landing and to the noise of flight attendants scurrying up and down the aisle.

As the plane slowly taxied, I looked out the window, still groggy, trying to identify the logos of exotic airlines I never even knew existed.

Strangely, the line at immigration was short. I waited behind two other passengers. The agent just asked me how many days I intended to stay in the United States. That was it. She took my picture and my fingerprints, and with a heavy thwack she stamped and stapled my passport.

By 8 A.M. I was in a taxi on the way to the hotel.

For someone sensitive to smells, especially someone obsessed with cleanliness like me, a cab ride can be an uncomfortable experience. I always brace myself for unpleasant odors. Food, sweat, gases—the possibilities are endless.

My taxi, however, was clean and pleasant-smelling. I sat in silence in the backseat, looking out the window, fantasizing about the lives of the drivers and passengers in the other cars. Some sipped from thermos bottles—tea, coffee, whiskey?—while they drove. Some moved their lips, as if singing or talking into cell phones. Everyone looked ahead.

From his license, I could see the cab driver's name was Dieudonné Pascal. At about the Midtown Tunnel, I tried to make conversation. I asked where he was from. He said Haiti.

He did not react when I said Brazil. We drove in silence to the hotel on 57th Street between Fifth and Sixth avenues.

Luckily, I did not have to wait for a room. Mine was ready and I was able go straight up. There was a message from Mariana on my cell phone. I called her and arranged to have lunch at a Chinese restaurant on 93rd Street, halfway between her dorm and where I was staying.

We agreed to meet at noon. In my room, I ordered coffee and bathed sitting in the bathtub while holding the shower head in my hand. I shaved, got dressed and went out for a walk in Manhattan. It was sunny, but not too hot. I entertained myself with the scenery and ended up walking all the way from the hotel to the restaurant.

It had been one year since I had last seen my daughter. She told me of her new job, of the apartment she was thinking of renting, her plans to go to India for the wedding of her American boyfriend's friend. It was as if we had never been apart.

I listened to her reasoning. We arrived at similar conclusions. I realized that my daughter was doing with her life the same things I would if it were my life. Our first conversation did me good.

This would be a short trip. I had to organize my time well. The graduation ceremony would be on Wednesday, in two days' time. On Thursday, I would meet with Cecilia Coutts. On Friday afternoon, I would return to Brazil. I would have to be fast. I could not wait for things to happen. So, right after lunch, I made the first move in solving the mystery that was bothering me: I went to see where Sergio's body had been found.

Objectively speaking, seeing the house in the West Village where Sergio Y. had lived and died should have made no difference whatsoever. Subjectively, however, the place where he had lived was an important element in contextualizing his existence in New York. I had imagined the type of neighborhood it would be, and even before going there, I could almost see the house at 12 Grove Street.

I thought of taking a cab but felt it would be more practical to go by subway. I got off at Union Square, and to enjoy the sunny day and remember my youth, I walked the rest of the way. On my walk, I counted down the street numbers and observed the people around me, block by block, until I arrived at my destination in the West Village.

Sergio lived the last four years of his life in this exposed brick brownstone. I wondered whether it had been his choice to inhabit the solemn building in front of which I now stood.

I passed my hand over the building's short brown wall. I looked up at the stoop. I noticed the detail of the stained glass window on the door panel. I did not get the chance to see the garden in the back, but I understood where it was located. I imagined Sergio on a snowy day, walking down those steps carefully to avoid slipping.

He died two days after a blizzard blanketed the city and cut off power for hours. This image of winter and sensation of cold came to me on a summer's day with students walking about the streets in T-shirts and flip-flops.

At night, I felt strange. I did not know if it was fatigue or the beginning of the flu. My body ached, my feet hurt, my legs hurt, and I felt very tired. Nonetheless I didn't cancel my dinner plans with my daughter and her two college friends who she wanted to introduce me to.

I had a pleasant conversation over dinner with Victoria, an Argentinian from General Roca, and Tatiana, an Italian from Milan. I had fun. I forgot my physical discomfort. I returned to the hotel and fell asleep immediately. I did not even dream.

The next morning, I woke up very early. I stayed in my room reading newspapers online until about 9:30 A.M. I showered and went out to buy a dark blue blazer, which I would wear at the graduation ceremony. I also wanted to buy Mariana a ring.

Next, I wanted to go to a used bookstore near Gramercy Park to look for a book. On the way, I would pass by 23rd Street and visit the cooking school Sergio Y. had attended.

I went to the main office at the Institute of Culinary Education. The information I wanted, however, was protected by privacy laws, and I was not able to find out which courses Sergio or Sandra had taken. The only information they could give me freely was whether either of the two had ever been a student (yes, both had been students) and had graduated from the school (yes, Sergio Y. received two diplomas, in 2007 and 2008; Sandra Yacoubian received one in 2009).

A blonde girl with a serpentine tattoo around her wrist handed me a course brochure. It recommended students start with a basic cooking course and then complement that with electives.

Sergio had to have completed three mandatory courses in that catalog. One would almost certainly have been a culinary fundamentals course to learn general cooking techniques and food handling. I had no way of knowing what the others were. If I had only known the cuisine at the restaurant he had come close to opening, I would have been able to deduce. But it was impossible to conjecture blindly.

The distance I had walked and the disappointment at not being able to find out everything I had wanted about Sergio Y. for the first time on this trip made me feel somewhat defeated.

I came to the realization that not only was he dead, but that his stay in this city had left almost no traces. His presence was fading. The city was forgetting him. In New York, Sergio Y. barely existed anymore.

Mariana scheduled a dinner with her friends that evening. I thought I would offer to accompany her, but the group was big and I would be the only parent. I decided instead to order a sandwich and a bottle of wine in my room and go to bed early. However, after drinking two-thirds of the bottle, my mood improved and I was full of energy. I went for a walk.

I walked north along Fifth Avenue, with Central Park to my left. With the fresh park air blowing on my face, I had a surge of confidence. At that moment, I felt I could still live a well-adjusted life. I would resolve my conflicted feelings toward Sergio Y., I would return to Brazil and continue to be a good analyst and a good person. I would avoid anything that would cause harm to others. Mariana would be happy forever. They would discover the cure for cancer. No one would ever die.

At around 72nd Street, part of the wine had already been processed by my body, and my euphoria began to give way to fatigue. I walked another three blocks before deciding to go back.

In my hotel room, I again had the desire to breathe a bit of fresh air. But the window had a safety lock, and I could only crack it open about five centimeters; it was not enough to let the air in, just to fill the whole room with the city's muffled noises.

Before going to bed, I lay my head on the sheets and allowed myself to get lost in my rumination ("A rich doctor's daughter is more likely than the majority of the population to graduate from a good American university, right? If I were black, and my great-grandfather had been a slave, in what kind of bed would I be sleeping now? What kind of work would I be doing? Would my daughter be studying at Columbia? But why think about it? Things are what they are. One's wealth or lack thereof is a matter of chance. So many people start off well in life and do not end up well. I think my daughter has taken control of her own life. I don't even need to support her anymore. She's not given to extravagance. Her boyfriend is in Chicago with his father, who has terminal cancer. I met him last year in São Paulo. The boyfriend has also managed to land a job. Soon, she'll be married, and my mission as a single father will have been fulfilled . . . ").

I woke up at 6 A.M. Partly because I was still on Brazil time but mainly because of my anxiety over Mariana's graduation and my approaching meeting with Dr. Coutts.

I wore a blazer, a dress shirt, a necktie and new shoes. Before leaving, I looked in the mirror and thought I looked elegant. Once again, it was sunny but not too hot. By eleven, I had arrived on campus. I sat on one of the green metal folding chairs that had been set up on the lawn in front of the stage waiting for a call from Mariana so that we could make arrangements to find each other in the crowd.

I finally found my daughter in her black gown, with her blue sash around her waist and a small green and yellow ribbon pinned to her chest. She gave me a hug and a kiss, said she would call my cell phone so we could arrange to meet after the ceremony and then disappeared into a throng of her classmates.

I liked the speeches and enjoyed being surrounded by people full of optimism and dreams about the future. After the ceremony, I accompanied Mariana to her dorm room so she could change, and from there we would go to lunch.

She wanted to go to an Italian restaurant named Gino's. It was far from campus and didn't accept credit cards. If it had been up to me, I would have gone somewhere closer. But because she had expressed a desire to go there, and since I wanted to please her, we went to Gino's. I knew why she had chosen this particular restaurant.

Neither of us remembered the exact location on Lexington Avenue. We got out of the cab two blocks too soon and walked down the right side of the avenue until we found the restaurant's dark green door.

A notice was pasted on top of a padlock informing us that the restaurant had closed its doors at the end of April.

("Out of business" was what the notice read. Afterwards, I learned that they had failed to renew their lease, and the owner, who had had enough, decided to give up and retire.)

"Imagine, it had been here since 1945. It was almost as old as I am," I said to Mariana.

"It was Mom's favorite, remember?"

"Yes, I remember," I said solemnly.

"Where should we go now?"

We went to a restaurant on the eighth floor of a nearby department store. I liked my main dish (spaghetti alla carbonara) and the dessert (tiramisu). After lunch, I convinced Mariana to let me buy her some clothes, and this did me good.

We said good-bye in the late afternoon. She agreed with me that I had no business being at her "prom." She returned to her dorm and I to my hotel. It looked like it might rain so I took a taxi.

I went to bed early. I fell asleep filled with a sense of pride. The next day I would feel ashamed, but, on the other hand, I would manage to learn more about Sergio Y.'s life and my real involvement in his death.

I woke up very early. Before leaving the hotel, I looked up Cecilia Coutts's address on the Internet so I could find it on my map. To my surprise, I realized the townhouse she worked out of was on the same block as Sergio Y.'s. The restaurant he would open was also very near Grove Street. The cooking school was a subway station away. Apparently, Sergio wanted his life to be concentrated in this neighborhood.

But why an apartment in the West Village? I came up with several explanations, but I think all of them underestimated Sergio's motives, which were anything but obvious. I speculated on his reasons nonetheless. One could be the fact that the apartment where Sergio lived belonged to his family. Oliver Hoskings informed me a Brazilian company was listed as the owner of 12 Grove Street, owned by Salomão, I imagine. Staying at a townhouse belonging to his family would have been much easier than renting an apartment on his own.

Confused, I thought of the neighborhood's history as the birthplace of the gay rights movement. But Sergio had already given me plenty of proof that he was nothing if not a pragmatist. His choice would have been based primarily on practical reasons. Some of the most beautiful streets in Manhattan were in this neighborhood. His doctor's office was there, too. It was also close to his cooking school. It was a good place to open a small restaurant. It was perfectly understandable that he would want to live there. I myself would love to live there.

The West Village had a tradition of counterculture and projected a bohemian aura, but it was also a neighborhood for the rich. Not just anyone could afford to live here. One needed money. The best houses, such as the one Sergio lived in, belonged to famous artists and lawyers and Wall Street bankers. Therefore, the only clear signal conveyed by Sergio Y.'s address was that he was still surrounded by the class from which he came.

To my surprise, what I later learned was that when Sergio told his parents he wanted to study in New York, Tereza and Salomão flew there and chose the Grove Street apartment themselves. They took advantage of what might merely have been a whim on their son's part to buy a pied-à-terre in the city. But the apartment was much more in keeping with the son's tastes than the parents', I think.

Salomão's lawyer handled all of the paperwork directly with the real estate agent after they had decided to make an offer on the townhouse's two upper floors. This was all told to me by Tereza in a recent conversation.

For Sergio, the walk to Cecilia Coutts's office was a very short one. He would leave the house, walk down the stoop, turn right, walk to Bleecker Street, turn right, then walk another block before turning right again on Barrow Street. He never even had to cross the street. Along the way, he would pass a vitamin shop, a stationery store and a small cinema showing independent films, which he enjoyed watching on occasion.

Dr. Coutts's office was also in a townhouse, on the ground floor. As I stood in front of the building, I could see Sergio Y. standing at her door. His finger would have touched the same intercom button that I would press. His hand would have grasped the same brass doorknob my hand would grasp; he would have pushed that same cast-iron and glass door that I was now opening. Exactly the way I was doing.

We were together in the same place, separated by time.

After opening the iron and glass door, I walked along a dark, carpeted corridor. I pressed the black button under the number 3 and felt Sergio Y.'s finger under mine.

Vanity almost pushed me into the abyss

Cecilia Coutts was much more attractive than I had imagined. Her lips were thin and her smile appeared sincere. She was approximately 1.70 meters tall and had straight black hair that framed her handsome features. She must have been about 40, which also surprised me. Perhaps I felt that since we shared the same patient we might also share the same age.

She greeted me with a handshake. Probably because it was supposed to be a hot day, she wore a sleeveless T-shirt and—impossible not to notice—no bra. After greeting me, she asked me to follow her. She turned and walked down a corridor. I accompanied her. On the way, she asked if I would like a coffee. I was never much of a coffee drinker, but I gladly accepted the offer. I felt it was expected of me.

We entered a large room with tall windows. This must not have been where she saw patients. I imagined it was a large office, where she read, made calls, wrote and I presume received guests.

In the corner, by the door, was a small couch facing two armchairs. A bookshelf took up the entire side wall. Near the window at the other end of the room, there was a wooden desk. On it were some books, scattered papers and a white laptop, which was on with its screen open.

Cecilia gestured for me to sit in one of the armchairs in front of the sofa, which I obediently did. Without a word, she disappeared into the hallway, returning with a mug of coffee and packets of sweetener. Instead of a spoon, she offered me a wooden stick wrapped in a paper napkin. She sat in front of me and crossed her legs.

I started by thanking her for making the time to see me.

"Ms. Yacoubian sent me an email telling me about you," she said with a smile.

She continued: "Sandra was always talking about you. It's a great pleasure to meet you. 'You're one of my heroes,' was what she told me when we first met."

I had enough presence of mind not to reveal that our patient's name change still sounded foreign to me. I did feel a certain discomfort, though, which, rationally, I tried to conquer. I policed myself not to use Sergio, only Sandra. For me, it was like speaking in code.

According to Cecilia Coutts, Sandra's was a clear case of sexual dysphoria. "A typical case. What was striking was that there was no inner conflict on her part in understanding her clinical condition. She very naturally accepted the fact that she was a human and medical outlier," she said.

She explained how Sandra had made an appointment to see her the same month she had arrived in New York. In her first session she identified herself as 'transgender' and declared a readiness to transition. "She told me she didn't want to waste any more time."

Sandra had told her that, at age twelve, while reading an article about transgender individuals in a magazine, she realized that she might be transgender herself. That's how she first identified what she felt about her own body.

"She tried to talk to her parents, but they became upset. Sandra acknowledged the embarrassment she had caused. From that day on, she vowed she would no longer raise the subject. Tereza and Salomão also never mentioned it again. That's what she told me. Perhaps she felt the feeling would go away with time. She might have thought that she would eventually surrender to what was expected of her. Or she could have just as easily committed suicide. But none of that happened. Angelus's example opened Sandra to a feeling of existential possibility that Sergio had never known existed. She became aware of that feeling of possibility thanks to you," she said.

I did not feel comfortable enough to confess my ignorance then and there to that beautiful woman who was calling me a hero. Everything she had said was news to me. But I didn't want to disappoint her. I decided that I would listen to more of what she had to say, because, after all, I had come to her office to listen. She knew much more about Sandra's case than I did. At the appropriate moment, I would ask questions that could clarify my doubts but without making my ignorance patently clear.

Cecilia Coutts explained that the psychological aspects of Sandra's dysphoria seemed to have stabilized by the time she had met her. They had eight evaluative sessions. It was around then, she said, that Sandra made the most references to me. With the initial diagnosis confirmed, she continued her treatment and then moved on to hormone therapy. Gradually, she fulfilled every stage of the process until, finally, she underwent her reassignment surgery.

"The process wasn't easy because it's not an easy thing," she said. "But with Sandra things were easier than with most patients. She understood very clearly what was happening to her, her condition."

Coutts went on: "She came to me already very well adjusted. She spoke about you with respect, admiration. She said nothing would have been possible without your help."

Emotionally, hearing all the good I had done Sandra brought back those feelings I had had when I ran into Tereza in the supermarket and learned Sergio had moved from São Paulo. Almost like someone trying to avoid a subject, I asked Coutts what Sandra's life was like in New York.

She said she was extremely confident and took her cooking classes very seriously. She had taken a basic cooking techniques course and then other more specific and shorter ones. In total, she attended the school for a little over four years.

"She had very high grades and received excellent comments from her teachers. They were unanimous in recognizing that she had a unique talent for cooking, and with their help she landed internships at the restaurants of her choice. By the time those internships began, she was already dressing and living as a woman, though she was still transitioning and had not yet formally changed her name. My opinion is Sandra did an excellent job at avoiding the sexism and prejudice present in the kitchens where she worked. The prejudice she could have faced as a transgender individual was neutralized by the enthusiastic support of her professors and the chefs in the kitchens where she worked. Sandra would arrive early, leave late and work very hard. She experienced no problems to speak of. In the end, the fact she was transgender was only further evidence of her uniqueness. It was just one of the many rare things about her. It was almost a comparative advantage."

As I listened to Cecilia Coutts talk, I heard echoes in my head of Sergio's voice describing Areg.

"Sandra received offers from all of the restaurants where she'd interned. They were the best in New York. Surprisingly, she preferred opening her own business. She had the money and the support of her family. 'Why not go for it?' she must have asked herself. That's what she tried to do. It was what she was doing when she died. Sandra was a person of courage."

Earlier, she had mentioned "Angelus's example." I imagined she was speaking of Sandra's determination to open her own business. Pretending to know what she was referring to I said: "I know. She named the restaurant Angelus." To which, to my surprise, she replied: "Yes, Angelus, for the book you managed to get into her hands. It brought about the most important epiphany in her life." She looked at the bookshelf behind her and pointed to the spine of a yellow book on one of the shelves, face level.

Cecilia Coutts's use of "epiphany" in her testimony raised my confidence level. But my fear of seeming ignorant in her eyes also increased. At this point in my life, I know that not all epiphanies are positive. Some, paradoxically, show us the wrong way, the one we should not follow.

Cecilia Coutts did not detect the stiffness in my lips. Neither did she notice that for a moment I lowered my eyes, feigning a deep sigh. While she described the hormone therapy she had prescribed, I looked at the shelf, just above her eyes, trying to find the book that had unleashed this revelation in Sergio Y. I almost wished our meeting would end so I might get closer to the books as we were saying our good-byes.

I could not make out the word "Angelus" on the spine of any of them. From where I was seated, I really could not get a good look. I knew that the book I was looking for was there, but my eyes betrayed me. Against my will, I kept returning to the outlines of Dr. Coutts's nipples visible through her sleeveless white T-shirt.

Just then, the intercom rang. A patient had arrived. Our meeting had come to an end. We exchanged business cards, cell phone numbers, and she said she would be available to clarify any doubts I might have.

I left Cecilia Coutts's office not having had the courage to tell her the truth. I was not able to confess that I had been unaware of our patient's transsexualism. I never managed to ask the questions I had intended to ask. My vanity had prevented me from revealing my ignorance. I was intimidated by her beauty. As a man, I felt physically attracted to her. As a doctor, I think this attraction disarmed me, it weakened me.

Sandra might have referred to me with great respect and

admiration, as her doctor was now revealing, but this was never apparent to me. She never said anything to me that hinted at this. Even when she thanked me on the day she told me she would be stopping the therapy. Why?

If it were true that Sergio Y. was aware of his transsexuality from the time he was twelve, he did not mention the topic to me because he did not want to. Maybe he was not ready. The fact is, he did not. It is no use asking why.

He never told me anything. But, from what I could deduce, I had played an important role in his accepting his transsexuality and owning it. For some reason, I had been instrumental in his choosing his life's course. Was I therefore equally responsible for his death?

The question remained unanswered in my mind. Still, I left Dr. Coutts's office relieved.

I had been acquitted by one judge, Dr. Cecilia Coutts, who knew about me and the transsexuality, said I had done "a good job" with Sandra. Given that Sandra and Sergio were two identities of the same person, the good I had done to one could compensate for the damage I had done to the other. I could not help but feel flattered and feel the guilt lift from my shoulders, even if momentarily.

That night, I ate sushi with my daughter in the hotel's Japanese restaurant. Back in my room, I took a shower and went to bed, but the sushi did not sit well.

I woke up a little after 2 A.M. I lay in bed, thinking, motionless, waiting to fall asleep again. I mention this little bout of insomnia because, if not for it, I would not be here writing this. It was during those many minutes of sleeplessness that I arrived at the conclusions that made me feel obligated to leave a record of Sergio Y.'s story.

That night of insomnia confirmed for me the importance of humility. Pride had prevented me from admitting my ignorance to Cecilia Coutts. I had been unable to confess my professional failure. I did not mention my ignorance. I chose to stay in the shadows.

But I am a doctor. And ignorance, to a doctor, can be death. I learn in order to save lives. It is what I do. If I stop learning, my usefulness in the world comes to an end. I must accept that I do not know everything. I have strived to learn as much as I can. But I have to continue learning. I must see ignorance as an advantage. Learning what one does not know expands life's possibilities.

While I lay awake in bed I had a revelation. That same night, beneath the sheets that were tucked firmly under the mattress, I, who never pray, prayed for my parents' souls. Without them, perhaps I would not value honesty as much as I value it today. There would be no reason for me to tell this story.

At 4:07 in the morning, I sent the following email to Cecilia Coutts:

Dr. Coutts,

Thank you for seeing me in your office yesterday morning. It was a pleasure to meet you. The conversation we had about the patient we have in common was very illuminating. However, I have to confess that I have not been completely candid about my knowledge regarding Sandra's clinical picture.

I fear I am abusing your time and your patience, but I would like to meet with you once more. If you can see me today, Friday, for five minutes, I would be very grateful. I leave for the airport at 2 P.M. Before then, any time that is convenient for you is good for me.

A.

At 7:30 A.M., my alarm clock went off. I got up and went directly to the computer to check whether Cecilia Coutts had responded. At 6:56 A.M., Cecilia had written the following message:

> Dr. Armando:
> I have a busy day today, but could meet you at my office before 11 A.M. At noon I have a conference at Beth Israel Med Center. Let me know by email if that works for you.
>
> Cecilia

I felt relieved at her response. I immediately wrote back confirming my intention to visit her "a little after ten." I hastily finished packing, I ate a cereal bar from the fridge, I took a shower and shaved. All of this with the TV on.

I left my luggage at the reception and went to meet Mariana to say good-bye to her at a café near her future office, on 47th Street. The taxi driver spent the entire ride—from the hotel to the café—on a phone call, which he only interrupted once for a few seconds to ask for the address.

I was determined not to let the anxiety I felt about my second visit to Cecilia Coutts's affect my meeting with my daughter. I succeeded.

Mariana told me about the work she would be doing at the bank. She would travel to Brazil on a regular basis. With a sly smile she extended her fingers to show me the ring I had given her on graduation day. She explained how the company would pay for her relocation to New York, and that I would no longer need to send her money.

We said good-bye with a kiss and a hug. I got into a taxi and headed to Cecilia Coutts's office with the taste of coffee and pride in my mouth. In the car that would take me to the next destination of my unknown fate, I allowed myself to be overcome by positive feelings, such as optimism and a determination to make things right.

As in Fernando Pessoa's poem saluting Walt Whitman, images of Sergio Y. appeared to me along the entire ride to Dr. Coutts's office. "Hey, Sergio, it's me, Armando. Remember the excitement you felt walking these streets, going to see your doctor, trying to change your life? I'm feeling the same thing. Remember the wind you felt in your face on those hot days? I feel that right now. I know you. We're holding hands." And, once again, I felt his finger on the doorbell, his hand on the doorknob and his body in the chair Cecilia asked me to sit in when I arrived at her office at five to ten in the morning.

I began my second conversation with Cecilia Coutts inspired by the courage Sergio needed on his journey toward becoming Sandra. Coutts wore a T-shirt identical to the one on the previous day, but of a different color. Her nipples were still there, leaving their imprint on the red fabric.

Just as I had not allowed my anxiety to spoil my meeting with Mariana, I did not allow my desire to interfere with my conversation with Cecilia.

"I don't know if it's a question of ethics or humanity, or mere professionalism. In São Paulo, when I decided to write to you, when I sought you the first time, what drove me was curiosity about the case of my patient, Sergio. I was motivated by something in between egotism and altruism. I wanted to know more so as to become a better doctor and, thus, be able to better help others. That was my original intent.

"You know that I enjoy a good reputation. This has always been a source of pride for me. Sergio's therapy was inconclusive as far as I am concerned. I would not include it among my success stories as a psychiatrist. Quite the opposite. I only managed to make peace with the results of my work with Sergio when I heard from his mother that he was in New York, with the prospect of a promising career ahead of him.

"His death caught me totally by surprise. But an even greater surprise was his transexuality, and that there existed a

Sandra in our midst. At no moment did I diagnose that. I suspected nothing. I committed a medical blunder. Technically, I had the responsibility to know.

"You say I helped him greatly, that I helped him find the necessary stability to allow him to transition. But I had no idea that this is what I was doing. If I guided Sergio toward Sandra, I did it blindly. I might just as easily have taken him in another direction, off a cliff. I didn't know what I was doing. You say I recommended a book to Sergio that led him to Sandra, and I have no idea what book you're referring to.

"I thought I knew, and I knew nothing. When I learned of Sergio's tragic fate, it made me afraid of all of the other things I didn't know. It made me afraid that I might take my other patients to places I didn't understand, that without meaning to, I would lead them to failure or to tragic deaths. That is not why I became a doctor. I do not want to recklessly drive my patients to death, as I might have done in Sergio's case."

Cecilia stared at me in silence and then said: "I'm not going to judge whatever inner conflict you may be going through. I can only speak of Sandra. I just know what you did for Sandra. I can only attest to the effect your work had on her. You showed her that happiness was possible. That her life was possible.

"It was while she was in your hands that she became aware that she could be more happy than when she was in São Paulo. You didn't lead her to her death. On the contrary, Armando, you led her to life.

"Sandra wouldn't have lived—she never would have been born—if not for the advice you gave her. Sandra's first friend was Armando. You allowed her to reveal who she really was. She had understanding parents, but she needed a friend to show her new possibilities. She was lucky enough to find one in you.

"Sandra was happy. She died because everything that is

alive will die one day. We don't choose the day we die. It comes when it wants to. There are people for whom death seems to come prematurely. That was the case with Sandra. You had nothing to do with her death. Quite the contrary. You gave her life. Her death was an accident.

"From my upstairs window I can see her backyard, where they found her body. But even then, when I stare at her house, understanding I'll never see her again, I still never think of her with sadness. Sandra died early because she crossed paths with a crazy woman who decided to kill her, just like that."

Turning to the bookshelf, she said: "You said you'd never read *Angelus*. Well, you can have my copy. Sandra bought it for me during one of her visits to Ellis Island. But I think this copy belongs to you. I just ask that you buy me another one online and have it delivered here to my office, so as to keep my library intact, O.K.? It's a beautiful story. It's what inspired Sergio to follow in his great-grandfather's footsteps. In the same way Areg crossed an ocean to find happiness in Brazil, Sergio crossed an ocean to find happiness in Sandra.

"We don't have much time, but I'm going to ask my secretary to make a copy of Sandra's file. I'm not sure whether its right or wrong. It raises some ethical concerns for me, but I think it'll help you work through questions that ultimately have to do with compassion."

She called her secretary on the intercom and then walked to the shelf and removed a book, which she presented to me with both hands. On the cover was a sepia portrait of a man in a suit and tie, black hair parted down the middle, set in gel, eyebrows nearly touching, reminiscent of Monteiro Lobato. At chest level was the title of the book that had changed Sergio Y.'s life: *Angelus in America: The Story of Our Father.*

Within minutes, the secretary, who I never did see, called her on the intercom. Cecilia walked out and returned a few minutes later holding a manila envelope.

It was almost half past eleven and I knew that our meeting had come to an end. She handed me the envelope and said: "It's not just evil that we do without realizing it, sometimes we do good things too."

As I left her office, I wanted to thank her for her generosity. The word "compassion" came to mind, but I never uttered it. I muttered a timid thank you instead, but I'm sure I failed to translate the extent of the gratitude I felt.

I left the Barrow Street townhouse without looking back. I entered a taxi and headed to the hotel. In the backseat, I tried to read Sandra's file, but I started getting carsick and had to stop. At the hotel, I only had time to get my luggage. It took longer than usual to get a taxi to the airport, and I was nervous about being late and missing my flight. In the end, everything worked out, and I even arrived a little early at the airport.

At the gate, I again tried reading Sandra's file, but soon realized the documents and notes it contained would do little to satisfy my curiosity. I had no interest in Sandra's hormone counts, or the best surgical technique for her penectomy. That type of information was of no interest to a psychiatrist.

What remained was Angelus's story, which I began reading as soon as I boarded the plane.

The first thing I noticed when I held the hardback book in my hands was the $29.95 price on the back cover. The book that had changed her life was bought at the Ellis Island Museum, whose existence I had revealed to Sergio.

Maybe my alleged importance to Sergio lay in this fact. Before I mentioned it to him, he did not know of the museum's existence. I suggested the visit. As a matter of fact, I gave him directions how to get there: "Take the subway. The Number 4, the green line, and stay on it until the last station before Brooklyn. The station name is Bowling Green. When you come out of the station, you'll be in a square, at the tip of Manhattan; go toward the sea and look for a booth that sells tickets for the ferry. Take the ferry to the Statue of Liberty, on Liberty Island. Get off at Ellis Island, which is where the Immigration Museum is. It's really worth the trip. Especially for you who like stories like your great-grandfather's. The ferry runs all day, and you can get on and off whenever you wish."

I finally began understanding my objective role in Sergio Y.'s so-called revelation.

That night, on a darkened airplane I read Angelus Zebrowskas's biography until I could not resist any longer and fell asleep. Back in São Paulo, after taking a shower and taking care of some urgent matters, I prepared myself a tuna fish sandwich, and I resumed reading in the middle of the afternoon until I finished at around 7 P.M.

Now, after becoming acquainted with Angelus's story, I can better reconstruct Sergio's actions, how he interrupted his life story to start Sandra's. Sergio Y. ceased to exist. He killed himself but his heart kept beating.

THE EXAMPLE I GAVE UNWITTINGLY

And you that shall cross from shore to shore years hence are more to me,
and more in my meditations, than you might suppose.
—Walt Whitman, *Crossing Brooklyn Ferry*

I carefully reread my notes on Sergio.

It became clear to me after doing so that in his therapy the references to New York were linked to a feeling of existential possibility that I, as a therapist, had wanted him to explore further. Now I understand that this, in fact, is what happened.

Angelus Zebrowskas's story begins in Lithuania, at the time under Russian rule, in a small village called Gekodiche, which today no longer exists. Zebrowskas's biography had been a joint effort, compiled by his stepchildren. It was based on personal diaries he had left behind so that his story would come to light after his death.

"I want to show other sad people who will come after me the way." With those words, Angelus Zebrowskas explained the reason for his diary. The book was released in 1995 in what would have been the centennial of his birth.

In many ways, the lives of Angelus and Sandra were similar. Both abandoned their place of birth to seek happiness elsewhere, under a new guise, one that offered greater possibilities. They charted different paths through an analogous process held together, in both cases, by a central axis of optimism.

Sandra's motives become much clearer and more justifiable when one knows the story of the man she named her restaurant after. Angelus was Sandra, and Sandra, somehow, was also her great grandfather Areg. They were all part of the same stubborn, lonely line who, in the face of adversity, preferred to believe a better life was possible.

Many manage to improve on the first drafts of the lives they are given. But for that they need the courage to jump off a diving board fifty meters high, blindfolded, not knowing if it is water or asphalt that awaits them below.

So, in the hopes of improving the reader's understanding of my report, I will take a small detour and present a summary of the book that inspired the journey Sergio decided to undertake. I will tell you those elements of Angelus's life which I believe are relevant to understanding the lives and deaths of Sergio and Sandra, as I have come to understand them.

I hope the reader will indulge me.

The first to depart were Antonas Kinklas and Jurgis Vytautas, who emigrated to the United States in 1904, made a fortune and inspired a whole generation of unhappy countrymen by their examples.

The idea that there existed a better life on the other side of the ocean spread, and many young people from Gekodiche and nearby towns embarked on the same voyage to Bremen, Danzig or Libau, where they would board ships that would take them to another world.

Unlike the Jews, who wanted to establish themselves definitively in America, the Christians of the region thought they would make it in America and return to Lithuania rich, with enough money to transform their lives, build additions to their houses, purchase a warehouse or even establish themselves in Vilnius, where life was better.

Five years after the first men left, the first women began leaving as well. The first single woman to leave alone for America was Anna Limiticius.

Anna had gone to the United States to marry a second cousin. Her departure caused an uproar and gave new hope to many of the young women of Gekodiche, who, as a result of the exodus of single men, had resigned themselves to the possibility that they might never find a husband.

Anna Limiticius was considered fortunate. Along with a passage from Danzig to New York, her husband had sent her a small dowry for a trousseau. In New York, she would continue her journey by train to her new life in Bridgeport, Connecticut, which she could barely find on the map in the church's school library.

Anna was followed by Irena and Paula. They were followed in turn by others, and then came the turn of Adriana Simkevicius, youngest daughter of Old Simkevicius, the tailor.

Adriana was not pretty. She had thick eyebrows, brown eyes and black hair, which she invariably wore braided and in a bun. She was pale and if she became even slightly worried or sick, dark circles would appear under her eyes.

She was sad. Her sadness was apparent. Yet she never complained or blamed anyone for her woes. Her sadness pained her. However, over the years, she had learned to ignore the pain. It was the natural state of things for her. It was like living with a chronic disease.

For years, she cried every night, not knowing why. At fifteen, she learned to control the crying. To stop the crying. But then she became consumed by the desire for death.

She imagined a cold, bluish death for herself. She would have thoughts of filling the pockets of her apron with rocks and entering the river in early spring, just when the ice was thawing. She wanted to die beneath floating plates of ice.

She was taller than the other girls. At sixteen, she was as tall as her father. One of her grandfathers was Serbian, and they said that was the reason. She did not like it when her breasts began to develop. Instinctively, she began to drape a woolen shawl over her chest, until the day she menstruated and decided to stop.

To lead such a life in Gekodiche, even if she managed to get married, even if she managed to have children, even if she managed to establish a routine like everyone else, meant she would forever be unhappy. She knew this but resigned herself to her fate.

But she had a life plan. She would live for her parents. After they were dead, she would help her older sister. After her sister was dead, she—who was very religious—would go to a convent to work for the poor. She would cook, sew, clean toilets, do whatever was needed. She would live for others. Dedicate her life to others like someone who had made the decision not to live her own life, even though living such a life meant she could not avoid images of that early spring night when she would drown.

Franciskus Zebrowskas, her suitor, had apprenticed as a tailor at Old Simkevicius's shop. In 1911, Franciskus, who had emigrated two years earlier, decided to open a small shop of his own in Chicago. The business prospered and he felt lonely and overwhelmed. He wanted a wife.

Franciskus's thoughts had turned to Adriana, among the young ladies of Gekodiche, because she was a good seamstress and could help him run his business. In addition, she was the daughter of a man he admired. She was not the most beautiful woman in the world, but that, for Franciskus, was an advantage. She was serious, quiet and hardworking. She was young, she could give him healthy children. She would make a good wife for a man like him.

As was the custom among the Christians of Gekodiche, a priest conveyed Zebrowskas's interest in Adrianna to Old Simkevicius:

"Simkevicius, you have to marry Adriana off. Carlota is too old. The fair thing is for her to stay home and take care of her parents. Zebrowskas is a good man. You know him. He will make your daughter happy in a country where there is a future. Where there are a lot of opportunities. Talk to her. It will be better for everyone. Then she will bring you over. Who knows, Franciskus might invite you to become a partner in his tailor shop in America. Who is to say Carlota won't get married there too?"

Adriana was almost seventeen. She worked with her father at his tailor shop. Every day she would spend hours on end concentrating, sitting in front of the sewing machine, immersed in her sad thoughts. In her spare time, she would read and pray the rosary, which was her way of withdrawing from life. Franciskus Zebrowskas was honest, and he was also an excellent tailor. The twelve years' difference between the two of them was part of the marriage of convenience package he proposed. For whatever reason, Franciskus Zebrowskas, at twenty-eight, was still single and wanted to get married. Not having succeeded in finding a wife to his liking in Chicago, his thoughts turned to someone who knew the customs and the ways of his homeland.

Over Friday dinner, Father Siaudizionis exercised his role as envoy for the groom in a sober and considered way.

"It is a new life that you are going to have," he said.

Adriana listened carefully and reacted cautiously. She said nothing. She showed no excitement. She also did not react with disgust or repudiation. After relaying the offer, the priest asked that she speak to her parents and only give her answer when she was sure.

That night, before falling asleep in the bedroom they shared, Carlotta asked her sister if she would accept Franciskus Zebrowskas's marriage proposal. She did not get an answer.

The name sounded familiar, but Adriana had only faint memories of Franciskus's time apprenticing with her father. She remembered him, but not his face. However, because she was devout, she believed what the priest had told her over dinner: "Adriana, my daughter, I know that you and your husband—

if Franciskus is the one the Almighty has reserved for you—will be very happy. Happiness awaits you in America."

Father Siaudizionis's words about finding happiness in America deeply impressed Adriana. That same night, in bed, before going to sleep, she already knew what she wanted to do, even though she had not yet formally made her decision.

Her analysis was clinical and rational. Her basic premise was that she was already doomed to live an unhappy life. She had an inner conviction that her life in Gekodiche, doing what she was doing, being who she was, meant unhappiness was inevitable. So much so that she had already resigned herself to spending the rest of her days serving others: first her family, and then, after they were gone, God.

She had never wanted a husband. She had never even dreamed of living in America. Never had she conceived of a life different from the one she had, a life full of misery, which she had tried lessening by helping her father, by helping organize church festivals, by reading the books that fell into her hands, while she waited for time to pass.

Suddenly, the opportunity to exchange a damaged life for another one full of possibilities emerged as a concrete fact. The marriage to Zebrowskas represented a kind of unexpected reprieve, one which held out the promise of a life happier than the one to which she had thought she was condemned.

Even if everything were to go wrong in America, and even if she were to continue to be as unhappy as ever, there would be no harm done. Adriana had nothing to lose. Franciskus's proposal gave her something that, deep down, she desired, but had always renounced as impractical.

On Sunday, after Mass, she waited for the priest to inform him of her decision to marry Franciskus Zebrowskas. When she retuned home she spoke to Carlota, who conveyed the news to their parents.

Franciskus Zebrowskas sent Adriana Simkevicius a second-class ticket on the SS Kursk, which would leave the port of Libau for New York on June 19, 1912. Pinkas Simkevicius closed his shop for three days so that he, his wife and his eldest daughter could travel to Vilnius to say goodbye to Adriana, who from there would travel alone, taking two bags of clothes and a chest containing her wedding trousseau, to her new life.

In Libau, on the eve of her voyage, she slept in a hostel for girls run by Catholic nuns. That night, around dinnertime, she met a seamstress from Vilnius, Helena Viriaudis, who was traveling to New York to work at her uncle's garment factory.

Given the circumstances, Adriana Simkevicius and Helena Viriaudis needed to become friends. The following morning they boarded the SS Kursk. During the eighteen days they spent at sea, they shared the same bunk bed and imagined, together, but each in her own way, what their new lives in America would be like.

Helena was optimistic and spoke often of the money she would make working with her uncle. She would work hard, but she would earn much more than she would be able to make in Lithuania. Adriana, who never had a penchant for optimism, was afraid that she had traded in an unhappiness she knew for another one she did not, but by then, already on board the ship, there was little she could do about it.

She had no desire to marry. She would do so because it was expected of her. Her mother had given her the necessary instructions and she would fulfill her duties as a wife with her husband. She might even get pregnant, but it was not what she wanted. She would accept Franciskus's marriage proposal as a hedge against the ambitious bet she was making.

On the day she reached land, Franciskus Zebrowskas was there waiting at the port with a bouquet of white flowers. It was summer. He wore a beige linen suit; she had on a thin light blue wool dress, too hot for that time of year, which she herself had sewn for the occasion.

It took her over four hours to be processed at Ellis Island. Franciskus signed the papers for her to be admitted into the United States. A justice of the peace married them right then and there. Helena Viriaudis served as a witness. Adriana Simkevicius changed her name for the first time.

It was the first of many changes America would bring.

Adriana Zebrowskas stepped ashore, her legs trembling from so many days at sea. When they arrived in Manhattan, they took a carriage straight to Penn Station where they boarded the train for Chicago.

Frank—as Franciskus was now known—was tall and fair-haired. He made a point of helping Adriana out of the carriage, and during the entire trip he showed concern for her comfort. Frank was attentive to her needs, and this captivated her. He was affectionate, but never to the point of taking liberties.

His small tailor shop occupied the ground floor of a building on Milwaukee Avenue. They would live above the shop, in a small apartment: a living room, a bedroom, a kitchen and a small sink. The shop on the ground floor had the same layout as the upper floor.

Adriana knew no one in Chicago. She conversed with the Russian grocer, a woman, and thought it strange that the German butcher called her "lady," which she did not think appropriate. She was never rude, but she wanted to avoid any unnecessary familiarity. At night, she would study English at the Salvation Army school with Frank, and she would correspond with Helena Viriaudis, who wrote once every three weeks or so.

Her days were spent in solitude, working at the sewing machine, but that did not bother her. She helped her husband care for the shop. She would keep house, and on Sundays she would attend Mass.

Frank would cut the larger patterns and take care of all

business outside the shop. There was still no appropriate place to receive customers. Frank visited them, took measurements, made deliveries and bought supplies and whatever else was needed.

Adriana, for her part, was responsible for the sewing, packaging and finishing. She had learned from her father to take pride in her work. She liked to think that any piece sewn by her hands could be appraised by anyone, no matter how demanding.

In Chicago, the fabrics were more beautiful and of greater variety than those in Lithuania, and she had plenty of work to keep her busy. Feelings of sadness continued to plague her, although the excess work numbed her somewhat. She put the sadness down to missing her parents and sister, and to her own depressive nature. She was resigned to her fate. Now she would devote herself to her husband. If their business prospered, who knows? They might even manage to bring her family from Gekodiche to the United States.

With Frank she led a balanced life. They shared the bedroom just like they had shared Simkevicius's shop: imperceptibly. They slept in separate beds and were only together as husband and wife on two occasions. She thought that maybe that was why she never got pregnant.

However, it was in Chicago, childless and far away from her parents, that Adriana realized that she could find happiness in her new life. It was there, in front of the two sheets of mirrors that lined the walls of the shop where she spent her days, where for the first time she saw an image of happiness.

There, away from her family, surrounded by a language she barely understood, her life still seemed like one of exile. At that moment, happiness for her was nothing superlative. It was something as simple as the absence of pain.

Sometimes, she would try on the clothes she had sewn, to experience how they fit over her own body. She would look at herself in the mirror and would feel proud of the perfect finish she had achieved.

However, the day she put on Mr. Hafner's black velvet jacket in order to check the shoulder stitching, she became aware of something much more important than the fit.

On the shop wall Adriana saw her reflection, her hair pulled back, wearing a man's black jacket. And for the first time in her life, the pain that had been with her from birth suddenly stopped.

So by chance, like Isaac Newton and the apple, Adriana discovered that dressing like a man made her happy. She was only nineteen and had her whole life ahead of her. For the first time in her life, the awareness that she was still young cheered her.

Father Siaudizionis had been right after all. In America, she had found happiness. Her discovery, however, was personal and private. She could not share it. She would dress as a man when her husband was not home. For that first year in America, this was reward enough.

Adriana became a happy person. In the mornings, after her husband had gone out to deliver the orders, she would wash the dirty dishes from breakfast and sit at the sewing machine for another day's work. She would look in the mirror and decide, then and there, which clothes would kill her pain that day. Sometimes, she would wear Frank's shoes and spend the rest of the day looking at her feet in the mirror. At other times, she would wear a shirt and tie. In winter, she would wear a hat.

The news was delivered by two policemen who arrived at the shop at 4 P.M. on a Wednesday. At age 20, Adriana Zebrowskas had become a widow. Frank was dead, run over by a streetcar near Lake Michigan. His body had been mutilated and was hastily buried on Thursday.

Few people attended: two clients, two suppliers, the bookkeeper, Mr. Zydrunas, and three Lithuanians who greeted her but whom she could not identify. After the funeral, Mr.

Zydrunas walked her to the trolley stop. On the way, he asked if she intended to sell the tailor shop. Adriana did not know how to answer. She thought she would have to do something with her life. Maybe she would return to Gekodiche. She did not have much of a choice.

Back at the apartment, Adriana lay down on her bed and slept until the next morning. She opened her eyes and saw a beam of light coming in through the window and hitting the wall.

In the morning silence, the light did not help illuminate her anxiety. Adriana still felt pain. She remained in bed until 9:30 A.M., crying, as she had in Gekodiche before falling asleep. She thought about her parents. She thought about going back to Lithuania. She still knew almost no one in Chicago. She had not yet managed to establish roots. Many other thoughts occurred to her; however, she was forced to get out of bed and resume her routines. She had orders to fill.

In a state of extreme pain, she worked in Frank's clothes: shoes, hat, jacket and tie. She sewed without thinking. She delivered the clothes herself. The Russian grocer and the German butcher who called her "lady" knew she was now a widow. The clients knew too, and they received their orders with faces filled with pity and did not even bother checking whether the pieces required adjustments or not.

She had already written three letters to Helena Viriaudis—the last one announcing Frank's death—with no response. However, just over a week after her husband's death, on a Friday, she found an envelope in the mailbox. The letter was from New York, but it was not in Helena's handwriting. Instead the name of Helena's uncle, Adam Viriaudis, appeared with the return address. He wrote the following words:

Dear Mrs. Zebrowskas,

I have received your letters addressed to my niece

Helena Viriaudis. I wish she were the one writing to you, but the Almighty has willed that our beloved Helena should leave us prematurely, a victim of typhus. To her dying days, my niece had only words of admiration for you and the quality of your work as a seamstress. I take this sad opportunity to add that good workers (seamstresses and tailors) whom you might recommend are always welcome in my shops. With the aid of Providence, my business has done well, and I always have room for people with talent and a willingness to work hard.

Sincerely,

Adam Viriaudis

The weekend following that muggy Friday afternoon was transformative. The news of Helena's death unleashed in Adriana an emotional turmoil that Frank's death alone had not been able to arouse. She had now lost her husband and her only friend. The two affectionate ties she had managed to establish in this new country had vanished, just like that. She was feeling more emotions than she was able to discern or process. Feeling so alone in a foreign country made her fatally vulnerable. She had to do something.

The following Saturday, in the morning, she gathered her strength, and she went to the bookkeeper's office to discuss how much she could obtain for the tailor shop. She signed all of the documents he put before her and received an advance of $300 for the inventory and the machines.

She did not want to take the trolley home, and so she returned on foot. She looked at the passersby and wondered what ailments afflicted those men and women. What passions, what fears moved them through the streets of that strange country? For the love of whom did those people work?

She arrived at the shop weighed down by these questions.

She ran up the stairs, as if she needed to use the bathroom. She opened the door and entered the apartment and cried. She cried for hours. She could not stop crying. She went to sleep crying. She woke up crying.

She tried to solve the problem with the only panacea she knew. She spent all day and all night in Frank's pajamas. Sunday night, though, was particularly difficult. As if trying to heal herself with a massive dose of painkillers, Adriana dressed as a man from head to toe. She even put on Frank's underwear. Nothing helped.

Frantic, standing in front of the mirror where she had seen happiness, she cut her hair with tailors' shears. Concentrating intensely, she passed coal over her thick eyebrows and parted her hair to the side with the help of Frank's hair grease, which was still on the bathroom shelf.

Adriana Zebrowskas observed the final days of her mourning dressed as a man. That was how she went out onto the streets. With male clothes, walking in the end-of-summer wind, a cold gust hitting her face. She thought of walking all the way to Lake Michigan, but instead wandered aimlessly all night, and when neighborhood prostitutes approached her, taking her for a man, offering their services, Adriana liked it. Strangely, she felt happy again.

That night, Adriana had been transformed. And now she needed a new life for this other person who had just been revealed to her, who had existed all along inside, protesting throughout her entire life, preventing her from being happy.

The sleepy clerk who stood before Adriana Zebrowskas at the County Clerk's Office was accustomed to interacting with people of all different types. It was not unusual for newcomers seeking new documents to come wearing clothes typical of their countries of origin.

New arrivals kept coming to Chicago. In addition to the Lithuanians, there were the Italians, Jews, Greeks, Germans,

Chinese, southern blacks—all types. That tall, thin man, with coal under his nails, had lost his documents. He was just one more immigrant who could not speak English. He needed a copy of his birth certificate. His name was Angelus Zebrowskas, male, born in Gekodiche, Lithuania, on March 19, 1897. That was all Adriana had to do: fill out a form and take a picture with the photographer on the corner.

That was when she discovered she could be happy forever—and she was.

With new documents that identified her as a man, one week later, she wrote two letters: one to Adam Viriaudis and the other to her father, Pinkas Simkevicius. The first one was a letter of introduction for her twin brother, Angelus, "a very skilled tailor, who received the same training I did at our father's house in Lithuania," who "sought employment at a respectable establishment and a better future in New York."

The second letter, however, was written in a different handwriting and it was signed by a Russian greengrocer, "a friend of your daughter's, the widow A. Zebrowskas," who, she regretted to inform him, "had passed away two weeks earlier in Chicago, a victim of typhus."

The following week, Angelus Zebrowskas arrived in New York. He brought only one suitcase filled with Frank's clothes—adjusted to fit Angelus—and the letter from his twin sister, Adriana, addressed to Viriaudis, recommending his skill as a tailor. Helena's uncle recognized Adriana's tiny handwriting and employed Angelus as a cutter.

It is not known how the news of Adriana's death was received by the Simkevicius family in Gekodiche. Angelus never again had any news from them. It was as if he had lost them all in a massacre, in a genocide.

Angelus worked hard and prospered. He married Carmela, a Sicilian with two small children, who, like Adriana, had become a widow soon after coming to the United States. In a few years, Carmela and Angelus had a clothing factory and three clothing stores. Angelus became a benefactor of the Italian community, which he fit into so well that after his death a stretch of Mulberry Street, in the heart of Little Italy, was renamed Angelus's Way.

Angelus Zebrowskas's secret was only discovered after his death, while his body was being prepared for burial. The subject was, however, quelled immediately. Carmela told the priest that Angelus had suffered an accident in Lithuania and that their marriage had never been consummated. She asked the priest that the subject be laid to rest once and for all.

"Father, God could not have given me a more dedicated husband, or a better father to my children," she said before burying the subject.

MY CONCLUSIONS AFTER READING THE BOOK

Now the ties seemed clear to me between Adriana Simkevicius's story and Sergio Y.'s impulse to leave Brazil for another country. For me, the explanation could be found, at least in part, in the unusual title of the biography found by Sergio on Ellis Island: *In America: The Story of Our Father*.

As I understand it—although I could be mistaken—if Adriana's story corresponds to Sergio Y.'s, then Angelus's should correspond to that of Sandra.

This parallelism would be the basis for Sergio's going to New York. He would have followed Adriana's example. He would have traveled to find himself. He took Sandra to New York, so that she could be as happy as Angelus was. Like him, he would become a bastion, reinvented in a new country.

Sergio and Adriana jumped off the diving board trusting that in the pool below—that in America—there was water.

Metaphorically, America was everything that they already were, but had not yet managed to be. It was in New York that Adriana and Sergio were reborn. Or better said, it was where Sandra and Angelus were born, because, in fact, Adriana and Sergio only went to New York to quietly die.

I walk the city and feel a little dizzy. I walk block by block. If there are no cars coming, I cross even if the crossing signal flashes red. I want to reach a conclusion.

How much happiness was there in the life of Sandra Yacoubian, who was killed on Grove Street? On the morning of the day she was murdered did she wake up thinking happy thoughts or sad ones? That day did she experience any joy in living?

The few times I have been to a sports stadium, I could not avoid thinking that every one of those persons—not to mention the flies, the cockroaches, the ants, the bacteria, everything alive in that stadium—would die. At different times, of course, but each in their own way would disappear.

It is obvious, but we forget. It must be some sort of defense mechanism we possess without knowing. It is like going to one of those hypermarkets on a Saturday afternoon and, in the checkout line, waiting, surrounded by carts overflowing with grocery, realizing that all that food will soon turn to shit. No one thinks it, but it is so.

This is more morbid than I would have liked, but that is because I need to remind myself—I have a tendency to feel immortal—that we all die at some point. Some prematurely, as was the case with Sandra. Others, long after their expiration date.

Death does not necessarily have anything to do with the deceased's life. Happy and sad people die just the same. Death does not choose based on your mental state or level of happiness. That is the irony. One day you are happily walking along the beach. Feeling fine, walking from Leme to Leblon. And, all of a sudden, you feel a shock in the middle of your chest. The pain paralyzes your neck. Then your heart. And you go blank. You are dead. You were happy but died just the same.

All my patients will die too. The fact that their death will be tragic, or quick, or heroic is mere and complete happenstance. The death of Sergio Y. was criminal and premature, but was it fated? It is sad that he died murdered and young. But why should it have been any different?

Even if the body of the deceased were able to retain fond memories of its last day, those memories are final, finished. Not one more letter may be added or deleted. There can be no editing. Nothing more will happen to a man once he is buried—unless they decide to move the bones to make room for someone else.

Sergio Y. considered himself unhappy. Perhaps it was the same unhappiness which Adriana could not excise from her body.

For transsexual individuals, the body, its physical appearance, is the greatest source of distress.

Imagine being a woman, feeling you were a woman, yet being seen by the world as a man. An invisible woman, that is what Sergio Y. was. Doomed to never be seen, to always appear as what he was not. Imagine you, a woman, with hair growing out of control all over your face and breasts, speaking with a man's voice, hysterctomized, with something hanging between your legs forever.

Angelus and Sandra were locked in a prison for years, hidden from the view of others, inside bodies that were not their own. One day, after a journey, after an ocean crossing, they finally managed to emerge and acquire a life of their own. The feeling Sergio complained of in his sessions with me consisted simply in his not being able to give life to who he really was, Sandra.

The role I had in achieving this happiness is hard to assess.

Considering that my only involvement in the matter was to instruct him to visit Ellis Island—or so I think—then what I did was very little. Just a random comment, without therapeutic intentions any deeper than that. Of course I thought his visit to the museum would trigger mental processes, but that was only because he was an intelligent person, and the museum is educational. I thought he would like Ellis Island because when I went I liked it. And there was also the whole story of his grandfather, who found his America in Belém.

Sergio might just as easily have decided to go to Ellis Island on his own, not because of my suggestion or anyone else's. He would have found the book that pointed the way to his happiness and offered him an example to follow just the same. As you can see, my participation in all this was minimal, as my friend Eduardo had already brought to my attention.

Perhaps I am refusing to take any credit for Sandra's success for fear I would then also be responsible if her happiness had not been so great after all, in which case she would have died senselessly with her face pressed to the cold stone, merely because I was unable to diagnose her condition.

People's defense mechanisms are very complex. Those of psychiatrists are even more so. I feel like I am doing the same thing I did when I deceived Dr. Coutts with regards to my knowledge of Sergio Y.'s transsexuality. I should have learned my lesson in humility. I need to understand that accepting limitations does not make me more vulnerable. I need to seek out the truth, even if cautiously.

As far as Dr. Coutts was concerned, my role in Sandra's clinical stabilization was "fundamental." Tereza herself in the supermarket told me unequivocally of all the good I had done for her son. She even thanked me. She said: "Thank you very much for everything you did for my son." She seemed happy. And, if she gave that impression, it was because her son was doing well. There is no such thing as a happy mother with an unhappy son.

Sergio Y. had his sex change operation in a foreign country, but he did not suffer for it. If his search was the same as Angelus's, his goal had been accomplished. But did Sandra Yacoubian really find happiness?

I arrived too late to get my answer in person. Cecilia Coutts, however, confirmed that Sandra had been happy. What did the parents who gave her life think? What did Laurie Clay, who wiped her life out, think?

WHAT SERGIO Y. WOULD HAVE SAID IF HE HAD NOT FALLEN FROM A WINDOW AND BROKEN HIS NECK

I would have gone to the restaurant in a pair of nice trousers, a dress shirt, a blazer and no tie. I would have gone alone, on one of those nights when Mariana had plans with her friends from college.

Sandra would have come out dressed in a chef's uniform, with a chef's coat and a net for her long hair. Atop the net she would wear a white chef's hat, the kind we see on television.

After saying hello, I would ask: "Where is Sergio? Do you know what happened to Sergio?"

Sandra would smile and say:

"Sergio and I traded places, Dr. Armando. I used to be your patient too. You just never saw me. I spoke through Sergio. That deep voice was mine. Now, it's me, Sandra, who is visible. I've been given a reprieve from my life sentence. Sergio still exists, but he is inside me now, hidden in the past.

"It made me happy when mother told me she'd run into you at the supermarket. I always wanted to see you again. I always wanted to tell you my secret.

"I never told you I was trans because, to tell you the truth, I never had the opportunity. There were so many other things to talk about . . .

"At first, I hoped you'd confront me about it. But since you never did, and since I still enjoyed our sessions and learned from them, I continued my treatment with you. I had nothing to lose. Not everything in life is sexual identity. Right?

"I think I was getting ready to approach the subject with

you when I went to New York on vacation. When the Bosnian taxi driver who drove me to Battery Park to catch the ferry explained to me why he'd come to America, I was reminded of my great-grandfather, Areg. Do you remember that I told you about him?

"I would have died if I had stayed there. I would have died if I had not moved, as I did."

"That was the explanation the Bosnian taxi driver gave for fleeing his homeland. That was part of my epiphany. And on the island, in the museum bookstore, of all those stories, of all those people, it was Angelus's life I pulled off the shelf. I think God spoke to me at that moment. Angelus's life inspired me. He showed me what I should do with mine. After reading his story, I thought: 'All right: that's what I need to do,' and then everything changed.

"Thank you for being my first guide. You might say that you taught me to read. Without ever directly addressing my transsexuality, you led me to the solution. Silently—without embarrassment, without tears.

"By the time I came to Dr. Coutts, I knew exactly what I had to do with my life. None of this would ever have been possible without you. You spared me from the suffering and the pain.

"It's a pleasure to welcome you to my restaurant tonight. I knew you'd come, so I prepared a four-course menu, especially for you. Each dish will be a tribute to one of your qualities. Never will these recipes be used again. They will last only as long as this tasting and the memories it leaves behind. It is a small gesture of thanks.

"The first course is a mushroom tartar, seasoned with lemon and *fleur de sel*. I've used several types of mushrooms, chopped finely and combined into a homogeneous mixture. The sauce is seasoned with only lemon and salt. This dish uses few ingredients and pays homage to your integrity.

"The second course is a mascarpone cheese and corn ravioli dish with Parmesan foam. I cut the dough myself and stuffed it by hand. The mascarpone envelops the corn, and the dough envelops the filling. The foam makes everything more comfortable. This dish celebrates the affection you show your patients.

"The main course is eggplant, on a bed of herbs, stuffed with chestnuts, cinnamon and curry. This dish seems simple but is complicated to make. The base of the seasoning blend is made up of seventeen types of herbs, that must be cooked at different temperatures. It pays homage to your interest in medicine and healing.

"The last course is the dessert. It is a blackberry pavlova made with blackberry mousse, shredded meringue, macerated raspberries and lemon thyme sorbet. It gives off intense yet light and balanced flavors. This plate celebrates your intelligence.

"I chose the following wines to go with each dish: Bourgogne Aligoté 2009 for the mushrooms, Riesling 'Nonnenberg' 2007 for the ravioli, Arbois Les Bruyères 2008 for the eggplant and a Champagne Brut Nature 2003 for dessert.

"Please note that there is not a single fiber of meat in this meal I've prepared for you. I wanted to keep death at bay. No heart had to stop beating so you could eat in my restaurant. There's not a drop of blood on the food I prepared for you.

"I wish you bon appétit.

"My parents have tried everything on the menu. Ask them if I was happy. If you have any more questions, ask Laurie, she knows."

I woke up startled. But I decided to accept the suggestion made by Sandra in the dream.

LETTER TO THE FATHER

Dear Salomão,

My name is Armando and I was your son Sergio's therapist during his last year in São Paulo, before he moved to New York. I am doing research related to Sergio's case and I would be very grateful if you would consent to a brief talk. I will make myself available on the date and time that is most convenient for you. My email address is armandoa@xls.org and my telephone number, 999-9734.

Cordially,

Armando

THE FATHER'S RESPONSE TO THE LETTER

When you asked to talk to me, I found it strange. It's been almost a year since Sergio's death. I thought: 'What could he want with me?' I was intrigued. Then, you asked me if Sergio was happy. Just like that. Even now I don't really know how to answer you. There are so many types of happiness, aren't there?

"I generated two monstrosities: one anencephalic baby and one transexual.

"When the doctor told us our other son was anencephalic, I didn't know what to do. I ran to the dictionary. 'Monstrosity': that was the generic definition the dictionary gave.

"But Roberto died soon after he was born. We still had Sergio. With him I thought we'd got it right. I always thought he was a normal boy. He didn't have a lot of friends. He was the silent type, but he was a good student, and his teachers liked him. At home, he was also well-behaved. He was a good boy.

"I have to admit his mother knew him better than I did. You know life in São Paulo can be very hectic. Especially for those who own their own business. I've always taken on a lot of responsibility, since I was young. By the time I arrived home Sergio usually had already eaten dinner and was in his pajamas, watching television or playing video games, spellbound, almost ready for bed. But I always thought I had a good relationship with my son.

"I think he felt lonely because he had no brothers or sisters, but, if you think about it, he was always surrounded by people: at school, in English class, at swimming classes, judo—he always had someone with him. He'd come home practically just to shower, eat and sleep.

"He was a normal boy. He was in therapy with you, but he was normal. You met him. He told us he wanted to see a therapist because he was having trouble deciding what to do with his life. What were we to do? We said yes. Anyway, therapy is relatively common nowadays. But I confess a warning signal went off inside me.

"After Christmas, when he talked to me and his mother and told us he wanted to live in New York—and he said 'live,' not 'visit,' 'hang out,' none of that; he said 'live'—it was a big surprise. I had a suspicion that something might not be going well, but none of us understood the reason he decided to live in New York.

"A few days later, he told us he wasn't who we thought he was.

"It was hard to hear from my only son that he was a woman, that he wanted to go to New York because there he could live as a woman, have a sex change operation, change his name, be who he thought he was.

"It wasn't easy to hear. I was shocked by what he was telling us, but I was even more shocked by the calm and poised manner with which he communicated his decision to us.

"The proposal he made to us was that we would let him live in New York for two years to do the sexual reassignment treatment with a doctor named Coutts. To me it all sounded crazy, but I thought maybe it was just a phase. We all went to New York, Tereza, Sergio and I, to talk to Dr. Coutts, who told us about our son being 'transgender.'

"It took me a long time to understand the nature of what Sergio felt, but I never turned my back on him. I gave him all the support I could. I was sorry for him and for myself. I would never have grandchildren. He would never take over the family business.

"It was awful when I saw him dressed as a woman for the first time. I wanted to rip his clothes off and find my son underneath those clothes, those painted nails, but I did nothing. Nothing. I just avoided eye contact. I kept my head down. I felt love and hate at the same time for what, to me, was a caricature of my son.

"That first time, I controlled myself. And I continued to control myself afterwards. I couldn't lose him. I asked God to help me to get used to that. That I learn to accept it, that the sight of my emasculated son, dressed as a woman, become acceptable to me. I thought of that saying: 'If you love the ugly, beautiful you'll seem to them.'

"Sergio didn't want to stay in São Paulo. He wanted to go somewhere where no one knew him. He wanted to be able to introduce himself as Sandra forever.

"I understood that. I confess I liked that he did his treatment outside of Brazil. Our company is highly visible. The situation could be exploited by the press, by the public. It wouldn't be good for him. It wouldn't be good for anyone. In New York, he'd be anonymous and could care for himself in peace. Away from the curiosity seekers.

"We bought that apartment in the West Village just for him. I sent him a monthly allowance, and he had credit cards to pay for his treatment. His mother would always visit him. He led a balanced life. He interned at the best restaurant in New York. When he graduated, I gave him money to open his own business.

"The restaurant would have been a success. He was a very good chef. He had the common sense of his great-grandfather, who opened the first Laila store. Nothing can convince me it wouldn't have been a total success. There was even a *New York Times* reporter interested in doing a story about the restaurant. It's too bad none of this can ever happen now.

"Sergio just wanted to be happy. That's why my son went to New York. He was looking for a way to be happy. He went there to make lemonade with the great big lemon God had given him. And he succeeded. You asked if he was happy. Yes, after he became Sandra, Sergio was happy. He was in good spirits, he had friends. As a woman, he found happiness.

"My son was able to turn things around, and he died at twenty-three, murdered by an unstable woman who barely knew him. A crazy woman, a human stray bullet. That's the irony: dying in such a foolish way after you've found happiness.

"But life isn't fair for any of us, and I don't have a monopoly on pain. There are people who've suffered a lot more than me. And they still manage to live, work, be productive. That's what I try to remember. Sergio's death was a great—the greatest—loss I've experienced in my life, but I have to go on living. He was happy, and that reassures me, it gives me peace."

ONE MORE MUSHROOM

I have tried to be as faithful as possible in my translation of what Laurie Clay told me when I visited her in prison. However, I do not know whether it will be enough. First of all, we were separated by thick glass, and the recording I made of our conversation was not clear. Second, she does not speak Portuguese. I could not simply transcribe her words, like I did with Salomão. I will report what she told me in the manner she told me and as I interpreted it, even when it might seem obvious.

Laurie Clay is serving a twenty-two year sentence. She was convicted of second-degree murder. She had on an orange jumpsuit when we met. I could see a four-leaf clover tattooed on the inside of her right wrist, and she wore her blond hair in a short ponytail.

To get permission to talk to her, I had to make a request in writing to the prison administration. Her consent was required too.

Almost two years earlier, Laurie had been accepted to study fashion at the New School. Laurie met Sandra the day she, Laurie, was visiting the apartment her parents had bought for her. She was accompanied by the interior decorator who would help her furnish it. She was intrigued by that tall girl, with black hair and a red handbag, who was leaving just as they arrived.

The next time they met was at a café on the corner of Grove and Bleecker, which, curiously, I now realize, was named Angélique. They drank tea and walked back home together. They soon became friends.

Laurie, an only child like Sandra, had been an eccentric teenager by Louisville, Kentucky, standards, which is where her family was from. She went through several phases, all of which she devoted herself to fervently. There was a vegetarian phase, when she stopped consuming foods of animal origin and wearing leather. There was a Goth phase, in which she only wore black clothes and makeup, and there was a mystical phase, when she attended a variety of churches and sects.

I think the truth is that Laurie enjoyed being onstage. From what she told me, every new phase meant a new wardrobe and a new lifestyle. Because these phases were relatively short, she was constantly reinventing herself, as if creating her own cast of characters, as if filling an album with pictures of roles she could play. She never could have imagined, though, that in this album there would also be photographs of a prisoner.

In New York, she was living out her omnipotent phase. She was young, ambitious, headstrong and rich. For her, studying fashion meant, above all, expanding her collection of aesthetic experiences. She would go out every night. The experience she was chasing was the one she had not yet had.

"For someone like me, who'd just arrived from Kentucky, Sandra was the epitome of the true New Yorker. She was six-two. Super elegant in her manners and the way she dressed. She never wore prints, just solids. She had style, charisma, great taste. It was the whole androgynous thing. I'd never met a Brazilian before. She seemed exotic to me. Sandra was very chic. In a way, she was who I wanted to be. The day she died, we were celebrating the fact that the *New York Times* had confirmed they'd be doing a story about her restaurant. I was proud to be friends with her, to be seen with her. I thought having a transgender friend was the coolest thing.

"I never meant to kill her. I never even thought of killing anyone. I interrupted her life and mine in a moment of madness. Because of one irresponsible act, I forever changed our destinies.

"At the time, everyone in my class was experimenting with 'magic mushrooms.' A friend of mine, who grew mushrooms at home, gave me a paper bag with twelve small red mushrooms with white spots on them. They looked like little strawberries. 'The active ingredient is psilocybin,' he said.

"I was curious. The day I got the mushrooms it was cold. On the way home, I ate the two smallest ones. I ran into Sandra in front of the house. We arrived at the same time. We went upstairs together. She was beaming. She invited me in for a glass of champagne to celebrate the *New York Times* article. I wasn't going to drink champagne. I'm really not into champagne. But, since the mushrooms hadn't really taken effect, I thought maybe it wouldn't be a problem if I just took one sip to toast with my friend.

"We were facing each other. She sat by the window in a high-back chair. I remember her profile against the darkness outside the window. I didn't offer her mushrooms because I knew pot was the only drug she liked. She smoked it sometimes at home to relax.

"Sandra was all excited about the article. She kept flailing her arms about. I sat there, right in front of her, just listening. I think that's the last sober memory I have of that day.

"After that, all I remember was my hallucination. I started hearing voices in my head. I was certain I heard the voice of God. He ordered me to push Sandra through the window with all my might.

"The voice grew stronger. He repeated the order. Suddenly, Sandra sounded aggressive, threatening. She was an evil being. I became convinced God had entrusted me with the task of ridding the world of that rotten fruit, and I wanted all the glory that came with that.

"I wanted to push her. It was simply a matter of having a desire to do something and then satisfying that desire. Like buying a pair of shoes or a bracelet and seeing no reason not to.

"I pushed Sandra with all my might. I remember her losing her balance, tumbling, with her arms open, falling back in her chair. If I close my eyes now, I can still hear the curtain tearing.

"I can still hear the dry, muffled thud of the body hitting the courtyard below.

"The next morning, I woke up alone, in my apartment. I woke up to police sirens. They'd found her body. No one came for me that morning. I took the two o'clock flight to Louisville.

"At home, I told my parents what had happened. They went crazy. We talked to lawyers, but there wasn't much they could do. I surrendered to the police on Monday.

"I'm going to spend a long time here. My life is here now. Life goes on. It doesn't stop just because I'm behind bars. But it's very limited.

"I read a lot, I'm learning to meditate. I exercise, I write. I have my parents' support, but I think I'll never have children of my own. Prison doesn't kill you, but it steals important things from you.

"I killed someone.

"I don't like knowing I have this power. Knowing this makes me aware of the immense responsibility I have. It hurts to know that I stupidly killed a happy person, who would have gone on to do good. I stole her happiness. I subtracted happiness from the world. I have to make up for that.

"My dad didn't like me being friends with Sandra because she was trans. When he visited me, he couldn't even bring himself to say hi to her. He said transsexuals were 'the devil's work.'

"That must have stayed in my subconscious. We really don't understand how our minds work, do we? You're a psychiatrist, do you think it was my dad who planted the seed that made me murder my friend Sandra? I don't know. It makes no difference now. I'm here now."

A MESSAGE DISGUISED AS AN INVITATION

D r. Armando? Salomão told me you wanted to know whether Sergio was happy. I appreciate your interest. I really do.

"I had a very hard time accepting that my life could go on without my son. But it will. Roberto, my other son, who also passed away, had already taught me this lesson. I think I'd forgotten. Now I remember.

"I'm ready to talk. Would you like to get together? Can I invite you for a cup of tea?"

IF I HAD SEEN YOU,
I WOULD HAVE BEEN PROUD

We met in the tea room at the Maria Luisa and Oscar Americano Foundation. I parked far away and walked through the gardens. It was 4 P.M. and it was sunny.

Tereza was there waiting for me when I arrived. We greeted one another with a kiss on the cheek. I think that from the outset there was a mutual feeling of relief that we were finally meeting. Tereza ordered black tea and so did I.

The only witnesses to what Tereza had to say that afternoon, at that table, were two teapots, two cups, two tablespoons, two slices of lemon and me.

"The first thing I need to tell you is that I'm only here because Sergio was happy. Otherwise I don't think I would have made it. Knowing he was happy when he died really consoles me. I don't know what I would've done otherwise.

"I know you're a doctor and you've seen many complicated cases, but my two sons, let's face it, had especially difficult lives. In my darkest moments, I confess I wished for their deaths, I didn't care how it happened.

"One was born without a skull and the other one with the wrong sex. That's what I produced. That's my contribution to the world. A shallow person might not understand, but I learned to be proud of my children. I'd generate the same fetuses all over again.

"Roberto was an angel. He was in this world for eight days and left nothing, absolutely nothing, negative behind. A pure soul, without a blemish. I wanted to be with him from the moment he was born. I knew he would die 'in a matter of days.' That's what the doctor said.

"It's hard not to love a son madly when you know he's going to die 'in a matter of days.' My only concern was for my sick son. My agony didn't last long. Roberto left us and never looked back. He left more emotions behind than memories. I did the best I could. I was given an anencephalic baby, but I gave an angel back.

"Sergio's death was worse because it caught me by surprise. It took me a while to comprehend it. I couldn't accept that, after struggling so hard to be happy, precisely when he was beginning to thrive, he should die in such a stupid, senseless way.

"After his death, I stopped calling him Sandra. So did Salomão. For us, Sandra was Sergio. The child I gave birth to was named Sergio. While he was alive, however, we referred to him as Sandra, because he asked us to and Dr. Coutts recommended we did.

"When I heard of his transsexuality, my first thought was that I'd failed. I was a woman who gave birth to imperfect things, incomplete things. My womb was not fruitful. It was malformed, subhuman, I thought.

"I didn't want any of this. I wish it had all been a dream. But we don't get to do what we want, do we? What could I have done? There are a lot of things we do for love. I carried Sergio—Sandra, whatever—inside my body. I never gave up on my son because I couldn't stop loving him.

"It was worth it. After he moved to New York, everything changed for the better. There was the sex change operation, which wasn't easy, but Sandra became an admirable person. I know he's my son, and I'm biased when I say this, but what she achieved as a person, and was achieving professionally, was very special. I think that, in some shape or form, this was a result of all the love his father and I gave him.

"I'll never forget one spring day when we walked across Central Park, to the West Side. We walked side by side, breathing in the spring air. It was shortly after her operation. Out of nowhere, she said, 'Mom, I never thought I'd be this happy.'

"Dr. Armando, it helps to remember that we did a good job with Sergio. Let's not suffer over him. He wouldn't have liked that. He succeeded in being Sandra. It's what he wanted. He was happy. He didn't dwell over his misery. It was great seeing him so excited about his restaurant, seeing her look so beautiful. Like a model. It was worth it.

"Some lives are short. Others start off badly and get better. Sergio's life was a combination of the two. We supported Sergio as best we could. We gave it our all. There was the physical distance. But that was good for his treatment, Dr. Coutts said.

"You never saw him then, but, believe me, if you'd seen her you would have been proud."

A DOG SPOKE IN MY EAR

I write from memory. I write events as I remember them. What I tell you is only my interpretation. I make this clear because not everything in my analysis is rational. At this point in my life, I am learning that often it is better to feel the answers than to hear them.

A week after my conversation with Tereza, for two nights in a row, I had a dream with three golden retriever puppies. The dream was as follows: I walked down the street with the dogs, and they kept getting tangled between my legs, and I would try to avoid tripping. And I sat on the floor of the beach house with the dogs playing around me.

They had red collars on with metal dog tags shaped like bones, with their names engraved on them. The first one was Sergio. The second one, Sandra; and the third, Armando.

It was an unusual dream. It seemed harmless, but it stayed with me. I even mentioned it yesterday to Mariana, before she told me she was pregnant. We agreed I would go to Chicago in April. By then we will know if it is a boy or a girl.

A curious thing happened earlier today. Someone on the same floor as my office left the door to their apartment open. I think I made some noise as I was getting off the elevator, and a dog came out from behind the door.

It was a golden retriever, very old, his face already white. He walked toward me sweetly, slowly wagging his tail. He was not a puppy, but his collar was red. Right then and there, I thought of the previous week's dream.

I let him smell me. I stroked him lightly. He sat next to me and I could not help but think superstitious thoughts. It occurred to me that that dog, who appeared out of nowhere, was the same one from my dream, and that he was bringing me a sign. It seemed pathetic to believe this, but I am being honest about what I felt.

From the same door the dog had come out of, his owner, a woman of about forty, whom I had never seen before, came out. She walked toward me quickly, gently shaking her head and clicking her tongue disapprovingly. "I'm very sorry," she said, approaching to take the dog by the red collar. "She escaped."

I smelled her perfume, and, for an instant, the image of a braless Cecilia Coutts came to mind.

"No worries," I said.

While she held the leash with one hand, I took courage and said: "I know this may sound ridiculous, but I had a dream about a dog just like this last week. Can you tell me something about him?"

She looked up a little surprised but flashed a smile that was part ironic and part benevolent.

"*He's* a she. A female. Nine years old. She's excellent company. A real buddy. The best dog I've ever had. Everyone should have one just like her at home," she said.

Apparently, she had interrupted whatever she was doing to retrieve the dog. Her body language was that of someone who was in a hurry and wanted to end our conversation as soon as possible to get back to whatever she was doing. Not wanting to inconvenience her any further, I asked one last question:

"What's her name?"

"Her name is Faithfull. For Marianne Faithfull. But we shortened it to Faith. It's easier to pronounce. And if you live in São Paulo you really do need a little faith, don't you agree?"

"Yes, São Paulo without faith is hard," I replied, trying to sound pleasant.

I petted Faith one last time as we said good-bye.

Back in my office, with my neighbor's scent and the three puppies still on my mind, I thought about what had happened. I'm not a religious or mystical person, but I realize that in daily life, faith does exist. Now, as I write this, I trust, without giving it much thought, that I will wake up tomorrow morning and have a full day ahead of me. In April, I will visit my pregnant daughter. In September, I will become a grandfather. Life goes on. I firmly believe this.

ABOUT THE AUTHOR

Alexandre Vidal Porto was born in São
Paulo. A career diplomat, a Harvard-trained
lawyer, and a human rights activist, he writes
a regular column for *Folha de S. Paulo*. His
fiction has appeared in some of the most
respected literary publications in Brazil and
abroad. *Sergio Y.* was the winner of the
Paraná Literary Prize for best novel.

EUROPA EDITIONS BACKLIST
(alphabetical by author)

Fiction

Carmine Abate
Between Two Seas • 978-1-933372-40-2 • Territories: World
The Homecoming Party • 978-1-933372-83-9 • Territories: World

Milena Agus
From the Land of the Moon • 978-1-60945-001-4 • Ebook • Territories: World (excl. ANZ)

Salwa Al Neimi
The Proof of the Honey • 978-1-933372-68-6 • Ebook • Territories: World (excl UK)

Simonetta Agnello Hornby
The Nun • 978-1-60945-062-5 • Territories: World

Daniel Arsand
Lovers • 978-1-60945-071-7 • Ebook • Territories: World

Jenn Ashworth
A Kind of Intimacy • 978-1-933372-86-0 • Territories: US & Can

Beryl Bainbridge
The Girl in the Polka Dot Dress • 978-1-60945-056-4 • Ebook • Territories: US

Muriel Barbery
The Elegance of the Hedgehog • 978-1-933372-60-0 • Ebook • Territories: World (excl. UK & EU)
Gourmet Rhapsody • 978-1-933372-95-2 • Ebook • Territories: World (excl. UK & EU)

Stefano Benni
Margherita Dolce Vita • 978-1-933372-20-4 • Territories: World
Timeskipper • 978-1-933372-44-0 • Territories: World

Romano Bilenchi
The Chill • 978-1-933372-90-7 • Territories: World

Kazimierz Brandys
Rondo • 978-1-60945-004-5 • Territories: World

Alina Bronsky
Broken Glass Park • 978-1-933372-96-9 • Ebook • Territories: World
The Hottest Dishes of the Tartar Cuisine • 978-1-60945-006-9 • Ebook •
Territories: World

Jesse Browner
Everything Happens Today • 978-1-60945-051-9 • Ebook • Territories:
World (excl. UK & EU)

Francisco Coloane
Tierra del Fuego • 978-1-933372-63-1 • Ebook • Territories: World

Rebecca Connell
The Art of Losing • 978-1-933372-78-5 • Territories: US

Laurence Cossé
A Novel Bookstore • 978-1-933372-82-2 • Ebook • Territories: World
An Accident in August • 978-1-60945-049-6 • Territories: World (excl. UK)

Diego De Silva
I Hadn't Understood • 978-1-60945-065-6 • Territories: World

Shashi Deshpande
The Dark Holds No Terrors • 978-1-933372-67-9 • Territories: US

Steve Erickson
Zeroville • 978-1-933372-39-6 • Territories: US & Can
These Dreams of You • 978-1-60945-063-2 • Territories: US & Can

Elena Ferrante
The Days of Abandonment • 978-1-933372-00-6 • Ebook • Territories: World
Troubling Love • 978-1-933372-16-7 • Territories: World
The Lost Daughter • 978-1-933372-42-6 • Territories: World

Linda Ferri
Cecilia • 978-1-933372-87-7 • Territories: World

Damon Galgut
In a Strange Room • 978-1-60945-011-3 • Ebook • Territories: USA

Santiago Gamboa
Necropolis • 978-1-60945-073-1 • Ebook • Territories: World

Jane Gardam
Old Filth • 978-1-933372-13-6 • Ebook • Territories: US
The Queen of the Tambourine • 978-1-933372-36-5 • Ebook • Territories: US
The People on Privilege Hill • 978-1-933372-56-3 • Ebook • Territories: US
The Man in the Wooden Hat • 978-1-933372-89-1 • Ebook • Territories: US
God on the Rocks • 978-1-933372-76-1 • Ebook • Territories: US
Crusoe's Daughter • 978-1-60945-069-4 • Ebook • Territories: US

Anna Gavalda
French Leave • 978-1-60945-005-2 • Ebook • Territories: US & Can

Seth Greenland
The Angry Buddhist • 978-1-60945-068-7 • Ebook • Territories: World

Katharina Hacker
The Have-Nots • 978-1-933372-41-9 • Territories: World (excl. India)

Patrick Hamilton
Hangover Square • 978-1-933372-06-8 • Territories: US & Can

James Hamilton-Paterson
Cooking with Fernet Branca • 978-1-933372-01-3 • Territories: US
Amazing Disgrace • 978-1-933372-19-8 • Territories: US
Rancid Pansies • 978-1-933372-62-4 • Territories: USA

Alfred Hayes
The Girl on the Via Flaminia • 978-1-933372-24-2 • Ebook •
Territories: World

Jean-Claude Izzo
The Lost Sailors • 978-1-933372-35-8 • Territories: World
A Sun for the Dying • 978-1-933372-59-4 • Territories: World

Gail Jones
Sorry • 978-1-933372-55-6 • Territories: US & Can

Ioanna Karystiani
The Jasmine Isle • 978-1-933372-10-5 • Territories: World
Swell • 978-1-933372-98-3 • Territories: World

Peter Kocan
Fresh Fields • 978-1-933372-29-7 • Territories: US, EU & Can
The Treatment and the Cure • 978-1-933372-45-7 • Territories: US, EU & Can

Helmut Krausser
Eros • 978-1-933372-58-7 • Territories: World

Amara Lakhous
Clash of Civilizations Over an Elevator in Piazza Vittorio •
978-1-933372-61-7 • Ebook • Territories: World
Divorce Islamic Style • 978-1-60945-066-3 • Ebook • Territories: World

Lia Levi
The Jewish Husband • 978-1-933372-93-8 • Territories: World

Valerio Massimo Manfredi
The Ides of March • 978-1-933372-99-0 • Territories: US

Leïla Marouane
The Sexual Life of an Islamist in Paris • 978-1-933372-85-3 •
Territories: World

Lorenzo Mediano
The Frost on His Shoulders • 978-1-60945-072-4 • Ebook •
Territories: World

Sélim Nassib
I Loved You for Your Voice • 978-1-933372-07-5 • Territories: World
The Palestinian Lover • 978-1-933372-23-5 • Territories: World

Amélie Nothomb
Tokyo Fiancée • 978-1-933372-64-8 • Territories: US & Can
Hygiene and the Assassin • 978-1-933372-77-8 • Ebook • Territories: US & Can

Valeria Parrella
For Grace Received • 978-1-933372-94-5 • Territories: World

Alessandro Piperno
The Worst Intentions • 978-1-933372-33-4 • Territories: World
Persecution • 978-1-60945-074-8 • Ebook • Territories: World

Lorcan Roche
The Companion • 978-1-933372-84-6 • Territories: World

Boualem Sansal
The German Mujahid • 978-1-933372-92-1 • Ebook • Territories: US & Can

Eric-Emmanuel Schmitt
The Most Beautiful Book in the World • 978-1-933372-74-7 • Ebook •
Territories: World
The Woman with the Bouquet • 978-1-933372-81-5 • Ebook • Territories:
US & Can

Angelika Schrobsdorff
You Are Not Like Other Mothers • 978-1-60945-075-5 • Ebook •
Territories: World

Audrey Schulman
Three Weeks in December • 978-1-60945-064-9 • Ebook • Territories: US
& Can

James Scudamore
Heliopolis • 978-1-933372-73-0 • Ebook • Territories: US

Luis Sepúlveda
The Shadow of What We Were • 978-1-60945-002-1 • Ebook • Territories:
World

Paolo Sorrentino
Everybody's Right • 978-1-60945-052-6 • Ebook • Territories: US & Can

Domenico Starnone
First Execution • 978-1-933372-66-2 • Territories: World

Henry Sutton
Get Me out of Here • 978-1-60945-007-6 • Ebook • Territories: US & Can

Chad Taylor
Departure Lounge • 978-1-933372-09-9 • Territories: US, EU & Can

Roma Tearne
Mosquito • 978-1-933372-57-0 • Territories: US & Can
Bone China • 978-1-933372-75-4 • Territories: US

André Carl van der Merwe
Moffie • 978-1-60945-050-2 • Ebook • Territories: World
(excl. S. Africa)

Fay Weldon
Chalcot Crescent • 978-1-933372-79-2 • Territories: US

Anne Wiazemsky
My Berlin Child • 978-1-60945-003-8 • Territories: US & Can

Jonathan Yardley
Second Reading • 978-1-60945-008-3 • Ebook • Territories: US & Can

Edwin M. Yoder Jr.
Lions at Lamb House • 978-1-933372-34-1 • Territories: World

Michele Zackheim
Broken Colors • 978-1-933372-37-2 • Territories: World

Alice Zeniter
Take This Man • 978-1-60945-053-3 • Territories: World

Tonga Books

Ian Holding
Of Beasts and Beings • 978-1-60945-054-0 • Ebook • Territories: US & Can

Sara Levine
Treasure Island!!! • 978-0-14043-768-3 • Ebook • Territories: World

Alexander Maksik
You Deserve Nothing • 978-1-60945-048-9 • Ebook • Territories: US, Can & EU (excl. UK)

Thad Ziolkowski
Wichita • 978-1-60945-070-0 • Ebook • Territories: World

Crime/Noir

Massimo Carlotto
The Goodbye Kiss • 978-1-933372-05-1 • Ebook • Territories: World
Death's Dark Abyss • 978-1-933372-18-1 • Ebook • Territories: World
The Fugitive • 978-1-933372-25-9 • Ebook • Territories: World
Bandit Love • 978-1-933372-80-8 • Ebook • Territories: World
Poisonville • 978-1-933372-91-4 • Ebook • Territories: World

Giancarlo De Cataldo
The Father and the Foreigner • 978-1-933372-72-3 • Territories: World

Caryl Férey
Zulu • 978-1-933372-88-4 • Ebook • Territories: World (excl. UK & EU)
Utu • 978-1-60945-055-7 • Ebook • Territories: World (excl. UK & EU)

Alicia Giménez-Bartlett
Dog Day • 978-1-933372-14-3 • Territories: US & Can
Prime Time Suspect • 978-1-933372-31-0 • Territories: US & Can
Death Rites • 978-1-933372-54-9 • Territories: US & Can

Jean-Claude Izzo
Total Chaos • 978-1-933372-04-4 • Territories: US & Can
Chourmo • 978-1-933372-17-4 • Territories: US & Can
Solea • 978-1-933372-30-3 • Territories: US & Can

Matthew F. Jones
Boot Tracks • 978-1-933372-11-2 • Territories: US & Can

Gene Kerrigan
The Midnight Choir • 978-1-933372-26-6 • Territories: US & Can
Little Criminals • 978-1-933372-43-3 • Territories: US & Can

Carlo Lucarelli
Carte Blanche • 978-1-933372-15-0 • Territories: World
The Damned Season • 978-1-933372-27-3 • Territories: World
Via delle Oche • 978-1-933372-53-2 • Territories: World

Edna Mazya
Love Burns • 978-1-933372-08-2 • Territories: World (excl. ANZ)

Yishai Sarid
Limassol • 978-1-60945-000-7 • Ebook • Territories: World (excl. UK, AUS & India)

Joel Stone
The Jerusalem File • 978-1-933372-65-5 • Ebook • Territories: World

Benjamin Tammuz
Minotaur • 978-1-933372-02-0 • Ebook • Territories: World

Non-fiction

Alberto Angela
A Day in the Life of Ancient Rome • 978-1-933372-71-6 • Territories: World • History

Helmut Dubiel
Deep In the Brain: Living with Parkinson's Disease • 978-1-933372-70-9 •
Ebook • Territories: World • Medicine/Memoir

James Hamilton-Paterson
Seven-Tenths: The Sea and Its Thresholds • 978-1-933372-69-3 • Territories:
USA • Nature/Essays

Daniele Mastrogiacomo
Days of Fear • 978-1-933372-97-6 • Ebook • Territories: World • Current
affairs/Memoir/Afghanistan/Journalism

Valery Panyushkin
Twelve Who Don't Agree • 978-1-60945-010-6 • Ebook • Territories:
World • Current affairs/Memoir/Russia/Journalism

Christa Wolf
One Day a Year: 1960-2000 • 978-1-933372-22-8 • Territories: World •
Memoir/History/20th Century

Children's Illustrated Fiction

Altan
Here Comes Timpa • 978-1-933372-28-0 • Territories: World (excl. Italy)
Timpa Goes to the Sea • 978-1-933372-32-7 • Territories: World (excl. Italy)
Fairy Tale Timpa • 978-1-933372-38-9 • Territories: World (excl. Italy)

Wolf Erlbruch
The Big Question • 978-1-933372-03-7 • Territories: US & Can
The Miracle of the Bears • 978-1-933372-21-1 • Territories: US & Can
(with **Gioconda Belli**) *The Butterfly Workshop* • 978-1-933372-12-9 •
Territories: US & Can